"A Frederick Forsyth for the twenty-first century . . .
Austin Bay has written a novel that is, like its characters, lean, gritty, and well-versed in the international
underworld."

—Instapundit.com

"*The Wrong Side of Brightness* is a taut, suspense-filled
thriller with real characters and serious implications
about the war of terror we find ourselves in."

—Robert Flynn, author of *The Last Klick*

THE WRONG SIDE OF
BRIGHTNESS

AUSTIN BAY

JOVE BOOKS, NEW YORK

This is a work of fiction. Names, characters, places, and incidents either are the product of the author's imagination or are used fictitiously, and any resemblance to actual persons, living or dead, business establishments, events, or locales is entirely coincidental.

THE WRONG SIDE OF BRIGHTNESS

A Jove Book / published by arrangement with
the author

PRINTING HISTORY
Jove edition / June 2003

Copyright © 2003 by Austin Bay
Cover design by Steven Ferlauto
Text design by Kristin del Rosario

ISBN: 0-515-13546-1

A JOVE BOOK®
Jove Books are published by The Berkley Publishing Group, a division of Penguin Group (USA) Inc., 375 Hudson Street, New York, New York 10014. JOVE and the "J" design are trademarks belonging to Penguin Group (USA) Inc.

PRINTED IN THE UNITED STATES OF AMERICA

10 9 8 7 6 5 4 3 2 1

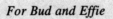

For Bud and Effie

"... from the wrong side of brightness ..."

—JAMES DICKEY

CHAPTER 1

My War, Her Murder

OUR UNIT REACHED THE EUPHRATES AT THREE THAT morning, a full hour ahead of the generals' war plan. As the lead vehicle plowed down the sand bank toward a line of river reeds, mortars moving behind the recon platoon fired two red flares, the flares hanging up there high, burning hard and long, arcing beneath the winter clouds in the night air over the water. The flares were bright, almost dazzling, and we could see ourselves in outline: tanks, men, the river, the world with a hot red edge.

And that was the moment. We stopped, all of us, and to a man, as if we were the same guy, we pumped out a whoop and shout that for a second seemed to stifle the idling whine of tank engines.

The whoops quit, the flares died. We looked at the muddy river out there in the dark that wasn't total. Since we were so used to the high-speed racket of a tank attack, those first moments at the river felt still—so flat, perfectly still—the clouds, the wet air, the world stopped cold except for the slow, molten water.

But hesitating there, strung out along the riverbank after our race in the south Iraqi desert, even as it happened—if you snapped to facts—you knew the magnificent sense of peace and calm was mental sham. Radio chatter from brigade, the tank engines, the sonic crack of jet aircraft, though numb ears ignored them, they persisted, and they are not the details of peace.

Yet the sensation of it, the stopping hard at the river with the killing behind us, that sensation was so decent, a change of immediate condition you knew was better, and if you've been dulled by the quality hammering you take driving cross-country in a sixty-ton armored can, a few seconds of stillness will fool you, bait you with enough fraud calm to get you believing in peace.

SHAM OR NOT, OUR BEST MOMENT GOT OVER AND done. A jet fighter shot low over the river channel, the orange burst from the aircraft's engine hurling a shock wave that snapped heads around. Radios cracked orders. The supply convoy, a dozen trucks belching diesel, pulled in behind the tanks, and guys, after pissing in the mud, started passing out tank main gun ammunition. That went fast—our tanks didn't need much cannon ammo, only five or six rounds each. It seemed we'd had more trouble with nagging rains and sand than trouble with the enemy. When the Iraqis did decide to fight, we used our high-tech and nailed them before they could see anything but the sand our tracks kicked up. We destroyed their tanks at very long range, the way we trained to do it, to get a distance, a good separation, stay out of their range, put them in ours, pull the trigger, and keep moving. These right kinds of victories were blasts of light on the horizon, flame, metal, bodies, scraps of gut horror as we sped past them to the river.

After the main gun rounds reached the tanks, the supply people started issuing rifle and machine gun ammunition. Wary of stray artillery shells and snipers— for there was marsh and swamp along the river, cover for a gutsy enemy—we shuffled through the cool, fading night, dodging big vehicles, lugging metal ammo boxes, the long links of belt machine gun ammo draping shoulders like loose, flopping chains.

Then dawn got us, like, click, night's finished, here's the sun. Supply had pushed up hot meals, and there we sat, in our armor by that Mesopotamian river, watching the river edge, eating freeze-dried scrambled eggs off Dixie paper plates. The air was wet, chilly, the paper plates hot on our hands. The Euphrates River was muddy, the marsh across the river green and gray, the sun red in the flat clouds at the east horizon. Behind us, where we had been, lay the low west edge of the valley and behind that so much Saudi desert.

The radios squawked with more orders. We gulped the food, swishing it down with instant coffee and bottled French glacier water. Our tanks were in gear again, driving east this time, the big swing toward Basra that, according to the Washington generals, would cut off and kill the Iraqi Army.

Someone in the trailing infantry company couldn't resist. Machine gun fire ripped across the brown water. Maybe there was a target over there on the other side and maybe there wasn't. The red-orange tracers cracked across the river, their trajectory flat and screaming. The tracers snapped at the green, disappeared into the green marsh and gray swamp.

An hour later, while watching the Air Force dump bombs on the sand at the horizon, we got word the war was almost done. We were back in the desert, just south of the lip of the river valley. Up ahead we made out an Iraqi airfield, a gray wrinkle of smoke rising from the fragments of a building. With this war minutes from being history, everyone sped up. Our battalion took the base without a shot, pulling in behind the sand berms on the far side of the bomb-chucked asphalt runway. The Iraqis had abandoned the field, but experience said peel your eyes for snipers and whackos, for damned sure watch out for more of the land mines the enemy's scattered over the desert. So we opened the turret hatches carefully, and as soon as we slipped out our goggled faces veiled with that peculiar desert dust that if the air's wet or dry, no matter, it drapes you like a powdered skin. Smoke from the burning building at the edge of the runway had put soot in the air, and with the wind slack the settling dust was grayer, a powder skin with a shadow.

After checking for snipers, taking a swipe at the dust, men ran out shortwave antennas, to pick up VOA and BBC on their portable radios, to hear that this swift war was over and done.

They all said it was finished. The President said it was. Someone said the Chairman of the Joint Chiefs was live on Voice of America, four stars saying it was kaput. The brigade commander pulled up in his tank, climbed on the turret and stood up, something you'd never see that careful, analytic man do, but he did it, and did it with a kind of joy. As a helicopter flew over the captured airfield, the brigade commander whooped it up like all of us, waved his arms back and forth, and the chopper circled the field, performing a victory wiggle.

On the radio nets everybody was saying that the airstrip was secure and tight, no sign of unfriendlies but watch for two unmarked minefields south of the runway. With the all clear out, many guys started shutting down their vehicles. The helicopter left, heading south toward the black smudge horizon where Kuwait's oilfields burned.

The engine racket of the departing helicopter faded, flat died. With the tank engines shut off the feel was spooky, for then it *was* still, the Arab desert silent, total whisper quiet until the slack wind suddenly gusted up, blowing across the level span of the airstrip. Maybe it was over. The Secretary of Defense said so on Voice of America. Thrive on the euphoria and triumph.

TWO DAYS LATER WE SHOT UP AN IRAQI COLUMN, remnants of that Republican Guards mechanized infantry division. The bastards were lost in the desert. We'd all seen the dust trail their column kicked up, that's the clue that broke up the card games, shut off the CD players and brought us into our tanks. In an After Action Report one of the junior officers said his men had beads on the lead vehicles in the approaching column but waited, thinking maybe this was a surrendering unit. The war was over everyone said, confused human beings were rambling all over the desert, don't shoot unless you're really sure.

Then a couple of Iraqi tanks fired and one of their

shells clipped a recon platoon vehicle. We suffered two wounded from that screwup, gashes from armor spalling, smashed eardrums and broken ribs. So the rest of us reacted like peace had been the split second it was. We performed, the whole battalion going instant at the Iraqis. Within six minutes we destroyed or captured ninety-two Iraqi vehicles, thirty of them tanks, plinked them like that, making smoke out of steel. The Iraqis abandoned their tanks and trucks, then ran into their own minefield, crawled in the sand right in our gunsights. We could have machine gunned the lot but we didn't. Though we weren't steady—and when you're in it you're never steady as you ought to be—our unit had that level of discipline, habits to curb fear and excess. As their tanks flamed they surrendered fast.

THE ATROCITIES: OUR EUPHORIA PRECEDED THE ATROCITIES.

Four days after that fight we were ordered to quit the air base and move back north and west to the river valley. This time, noontime and tired, where we stopped on the river we could see a village on the far bank, a Shiite Arab farmer village in the marshes maybe a kilometer away. It wasn't much of a village, one-story structures, thatch, Sumerian mud, corrugate metal, TV and short-wave antennas topping the thatch like odd wires from the present poking out of the past. Observing the homes and people through the ballistic sight on the tank brought them to you. Some of the villagers waved at us and we waved back.

Three Arab boys crossed the river in a saffron-yellow life raft. Two of the Arab farm kids were thin and dark-haired, grins big as they beached the rubber raft and clambered through the red and gray mud. The third was taller, with a swimmer's muscular shoulders, a shock of curling black hair and not much of a grin on his square jock's head. We fed the boys the junk they craved. The young men guzzled cherry Kool-Aid and downed dozens of midget Tootsie Rolls. The Arab kids gave a couple of the sergeants small bags of dates and the big kid gave me a palm-sized tin of honeyed figs, two Arabic phrases printed on the tin, across the top an invocation that God is living, along the bottom a florid line of pre-Koranic tradition I translated as "Heaven's magnificence, sweet bodied as air in the Hanging Gardens of high Babylon."

I dropped the tin into my pocket and spoke to the teenagers. They came from the village. The whole village was happy, pumped up, in awe of the American Army that kicked Saddam. All three boys spoke a little English, the big kid pretty fluent. In a matter-of-fact voice he said his name was Abdul and he listened daily to the BBC. One of the other boys said he had a brother who fixed planes for the Iraqi Air Force, and he hadn't seen his brother in a year. Would his brother come home now? The young men peppered us with other questions. Where are you from—New York City, Texas, California? They asked me where I learned such excellent Arabic. They asked us when we'd come across the river and when would we kill Saddam? Sergeant Benski, the gunner on my tank, gave each of the boys a can of Pepsi Cola.

The battalion commander and I had one of the sergeants pass the word to the troops to be nice to the kids, but don't eat the dates they'd brought until the medics checked them out. Better yet, smile, be kind, but don't eat anything off the river, ever. Intel said that the farmers in the village had declared themselves free of Baghdad and Saddam. The farmers were rebels, ready to shoot it up with Baghdad, but even if the dates and sweet figs weren't booby-trapped with toxins, soldiers shouldn't take the risk. Treat the boys well, give 'em a hat, Tootsie Rolls, then send them back across the river.

I remember a couple of clouds appeared on the horizon, blue and low. Weather said the storm wasn't another *shamal*, at worst a scattered rain that wouldn't affect air and ground ops. But the clouds worried the kids, particularly their leader, Abdul. The boys boarded their raft, our gift camouflage hats plopped on their heads, Abdul in the stern guiding the rubber boat downstream with the brown current. They waved and yelled and we yelled back. What a great day, a solid way to end it.

BUT THE NEXT MORNING—GOD, FORGIVE US.

The intel officer showed me the report just before he dropped it on the battalion commander.

That damned morning. Minutes after the report arrived, we identified Iraqi armored personnel carriers on the far side of the river, at the edge of the village. The intel update had said they might be coming but there was no if, now, no could be. We watched through long-range lenses as the army we had just defeated (elements of Republican Guards Armored Division Hammurabi and Motorized Infantry Division Nebuchadnezzar) quickly swept into the farm village. Some of the farmers, the women and kids scattered, a few darting west along the riverbank into the marsh. The Republican Guard started to burn the thatch and corrugate houses, firing their automatic rifles into the air, putting a burst into a hut, pushing farm kids into a truck. Now one of the personnel carriers moved to the edge of the village and fired a long stream of heavy machine gun rounds into the marsh, the green tracers smashing the riverbank, rounds slamming into mud, rounds kicking up white geysers in the brown river. We wanted to shoot back, every one of us. Our battalion commander, you could see it steel his round face. I ran up to him. No, dammit, get back in your tank, Ford. Dammit, Ford, you can't argue this one. Christ. It would have been easy, so easy to open up at once and stop them cold. We could have done it at stand-off range with our direct-fire weapons or crossed that river and handled it face-to-face. The criminal bastards would have run and this time we'd have shot them in the back as they ran. We were ready, willing, Lord forgive us we were so able and willing. But the war was over, Washington said, Washington had said it was. In the face of murder and rape they wouldn't let us shoot back since it was done—

Private First-Class R. B. Guyton, the loader on my battalion operations officer's tank, lay prone on the top of the turret. He leaned forward, elbow braced, staring into his camera sight, his brown fingers coolly adjusting the big black seventy-millimeter zoom lens he'd won in a poker game. He pointed that pro photographer's camera rig across the river at the village.

"Major Ford," Sergeant Benski muttered over the tank intercom. "Th' hell we doing here?" Benski was in the turret in his gunner's seat, and, from the lay of our tank's main gun, Ben must've been watching the murder in his high-resolution ballistic sight.

I didn't reply.

Through my binoculars, sitting on my butt on top of the commander's hatch, I saw an Iraqi Republican Guard officer and this guy, a slender man wearing sunglasses and what looked like a gray jumpsuit, raise their automatic pistols. I saw them shoot a black-haired woman dressed in nurse's whites — yeah, nurse's whites and a startling face — then fire at two old men in the mud street of that village. The old men fell over the woman's body. The guy in the jumpsuit walked up to the bodies, a jivey, too easy walk, not fast, and he fired again, execution shots where the bodies lurch with the bullets' impact.

I bit into my tongue. I bit so hard the medics had to swab the damn thing with peroxide.

CHAPTER 2

BECAUSE THE FACTS REEK AND THE TRUTH IS SO ROT-
ten, I've invented alternative facts and preferable truths.

My fantasy revisions of history always start at the
point I bite into my tongue. Each lie follows the same
basic script: instead of sitting there, watching, I do what
every soldier out there on the river line wanted to do. I
reject the orders; I pull the triggers; I end the murder.

In these lies I bite my tongue, but instead of reaching
for peroxide and swabs, I slip down into the tank turret.
As I check the ammo feed into the co-ax machine gun I
order Sergeant Benski to vacate the gunner's seat. Ben's
confused, but he obeys. As he leaves the gunner's seat,
I ask him if there's a sabot round in the main gun cham-
ber and Ben says yes sir. Now he starts to get the picture. Ben wants to stay, stay and do it, but I order him
and RB off the rank. Beat it. Private Ward, our driver, is

over in the headquarters track, so I don't have to worry about implicating him.

I slide into the gunner's seat, adjust the control handles, make sure the triggers are set on co-axial machine gun, then peer into the sight. I pick up the Iraqi lieutenant-colonel and the jumpsuit in the sight, magnification shrinking the fifteen hundred meters between us. I squeeze the trigger. Machine gun tracer burnout is around eight hundred meters, but in the gun sight I can follow the hits of falling shot, see the dancing strikes on the ground in front of my targets. A movement with the wrists—I adjust the aim as I squeeze the trigger, and simultaneously the turret traverses and the machine gun spits and I walk the stream of lead into the two killers. They look up in shock, suddenly aware of ricochets, of the hard buzz of bullets. Jumpsuit turns to run. Three four five slugs chew, devour his back. He topples. The Guard colonel goes prone. He's in the mud; I can't see him. Then the Guard colonel springs up, a mud man. Bad decision. I fire. He falls.

In this unsatisfying lie, in this exercise, I have all the time I need to mete out justice. There are pressures in this lie, however, pressures to give the lie some of the feel of the real, complex planet. I know the battalion commander is on his way. Oh yes, I forgot to mention that before I slipped into the gunner's seat I turned off the radio. See, in the lie the radio's off. The battalion commander, Lieutenant Colonel Garza, has to come to my tank to stop me. If he gives countermanding orders on the radio I can't hear them, for in the lie I can only hear myself.

I flip to main gun and lay the tank cannon on the Iraqi personnel carrier. I peer into the sight. The Iraqi guardsmen are figuring it out. They've quit shooting children. I check the laser range finder. At this range, the personnel carrier is a gray and brown duck, sitting there, stationary between two burning huts. I squeeze the trigger; the tank lurches. The sabot round travels the eighteen hundred meters in a second, a red jolt of tungsten lightning moving too fast for the mind to sense the strike of the shot. But I see the result, the rupturing flash, the explosion.

I switch back to co-ax, grip the trigger, but now, after the intense avenging acts, I start to lose my grip. The lie begins to break. I lose the certainty of my weapons. The battalion commander slides into the turret, his round face outraged. Lieutenant Colonel Garza can't believe it. Bob Garza slides into the turret, cursing, invoking Christ and Mary. His lines: Pete, what's come over you? Do you know what you've done? Wait—stop it there. That doesn't sound like Bob. My lie can't diss a man like Garza. I get to strike back; he has to sort it out. So Bob draws better lines, church Latin, and spontaneous Spanish outbursts.

In the responsible lie Bob says "You're under arrest, Major Ford, you know?" In a less responsible version he says something like "Thank God you did it. Now, you got the guts to pay for it?" Bob Garza believes in discipline. He damn well believes his troops should obey orders. He also knows murder when he sees it. In all alternative histories, in each lie, Bob's trapped just like I'm trapped.

I'm out of the tank now, the firefight's over. The investigation begins. Garza says "We'll say it's an accidental discharge of the main gun." Guyton and Benski sign a statement that I ordered them out of the turret when I discovered that a main gun round was locked in the breech. We pile on a lot of technical jargon. The Star Trek generation buys it.

Hey, the story has possibilities. Except it didn't happen.

The next version. In the next version we try to create a more sophisticated, durable cover-up. The battalion reports that I thought the Iraqi personnel carrier intended to fire across the river on American troops. A board of inquiry follows, and . . .

No. *God.* That breaks. Everyone saw the targets were old men and children.

A board of inquiry. The investigation busts my cover-up. I get court-martialed and convicted. The defense attorney suggests conspirators at the top want me hung. The prosecution says I've put world peace in jeopardy.

In the finale I stare at the floor. As I stand up I say, "Imagine this. It's March 1945, not March 1991. I get orders to stop two klicks from a camp in Germany. My recon platoon tells me SS Guards are killing Jews in that camp. Do I sit still or do I obey orders?" I turn toward the television cameras. Or perhaps I whirl—if I'm a lousy actor with a lousy director, I whirl.

There are other possible wind-ups, but they become even more purplish and frail. Let's say, as this lie finishes, I ignore the cameras and simply flop back down into the defendant's chair. Instead of being jailed, a four-star general asks me to resign. Yes, that's the ending, resignation. After that I zip my lip. Or maybe I drift off, down a slow, muddy, croc-infested river on an inflatable raft, lulled by the relentless buzz of insects . . .

ALL OF THESE LIES ARE INADEQUATE BECAUSE THEY
are fantasy. They are not the truth. They are lies I tell to
cover a moral dereliction of duty.

At the river, I bit my tongue and followed orders and
the medics washed it with peroxide. While the Republican Guard destroyed that village and the executioner in
the jumpsuit carried out his crime, we sat and watched. I
watched murder, the blunt, brutal action right there in
my gunsights. I considered violating the orders, but the
dirt truth is I didn't. I didn't do anything except bite my
tongue. I was disciplined, I was the trained and disciplined soldier, and we were all so trained and disciplined
we were paralyzed.

God forgive me.

CHAPTER 3

A WEEK AFTER THE ATROCITIES AT THE RIVER, AS I left an operations meeting at division headquarters, the commanding general's aide walked up and said the boss wanted to see me.

"Is it about the war crimes report?" I asked.

The aide shrugged.

I went over to Major General McCullar's command trailer. He was inside, sitting at his desk, watching a live television news feed on a monitor in the wall of the van. He punched the remote control, put the TV on mute, and told me to take a seat. Yes, he'd read my After Action Report. The murdered nurse? McCullar told me I'd been graphic and detailed.

A glint in McCullar's eyes indicated he just might know why the nurse's murder burned. He'd been around awhile. "I'm supporting your recommendation to pursue a war crimes investigation," he said. "We've your photos, witnesses, everything it takes."

Then he said the order to stand by our guns and wait had eaten him alive. "It's a bad set of facts, Pete." He ran his left hand over his close-cropped silver hair. McCullar had his BDU sleeves rolled up. I could see the long, hollow scoop of scar tissue and skin that functions as his right forearm. "Don't forget this, Pete. It's better if you don't forget. Failure should motivate us to make better facts."

I nodded.

McCullar nodded. I thought that finished it, but he raised his head and asked, "Now . . . have you decided what you want to do with Dr. Gunther's job offer?"

McCullar read my reaction dead on. "It's no secret, Pete. I've heard from three different people." He anticipated my counterquestion and raised three fingers: "Major Ted Nicholson, in Corps G-2. The Corps commander. And Ambassador Kilean."

I knew McCullar knew Kilean; it seemed, at some point, everybody met Kilean. Talking to Kilean might explain the glint in McCullar's eye when he mentioned the nurse.

I asked General McCullar when he last spoke to Kilean.

"The day I decided to ask CENTCOM to let you serve in this division," McCullar replied.

I said, too rashly, that I didn't know Kilean had fixed the transfer.

"He didn't fix it. Getting you into this division is a plus. . . . Have you talked to Ambassador Kilean about the murders?"

"No sir."

"How come? He can certainly help with a war crimes investigation."

"He's a *back* channel contact, sir. I want to make the system work before . . . before I go back channel. Why don't you send him a copy of my report?"

"Yeah," McCullar nodded, "you're doing it right. I'll send him a copy of my comments, too." General McCullar paused, reflected a moment, then leaned forward. "Pete, listen to me. Here's why I wanted to talk to you." He paused again, made sure we had eye contact. "Please don't decide to quit the Army while you're angry. Okay? With the Cold War done, we absolutely have to have soldiers with your skill package. You know the new game, it's murkier, more political. We *must* have soldiers who can operate in the environment, or we're going to get hurt. We may get hurt anyway. You know there are dirty players out there."

McCullar reached into his shirt pocket and pulled out his reading glasses. He opened the gold frames carefully, slipped them on his face. Once he had the glasses on he said, with the kind of sigh that indicated he thought I'd made up my mind, "*But* . . . NGOs like Gunther's can't operate without good people, either. He's smart. He's got a Nobel. And he knows you."

I said, evenly, "My mother worked with Dr. Gunther."

"Kilean told me."

"I haven't made a decision."

"Then let's talk again," McCullar replied.

TED NICHOLSON, STICKING HIS BIG UNGAINLY NOSE IN.
Ted—known both as Terrible Teddy and Pudge to his

friends and enemies—had a big, hulking body, a long schnozz that didn't quite fit his face and a full set of lengthy, dextrous, busy fingers attached to a twelve-cylinder brain. He spoke four languages fluently, and had a master's from The Fletcher School. He was also a calculated gossip. Discussing Gunther's job offer with the Corps Commander and McCullar—classic Nicholson, words placed like pinpoint smart bombs. Ted wanted me to stay in the Army, that's why he chatted up McCullar. Nicholson, like me, had foreign liaison officer and military attaché time, and Ted, seeking to flatter as much as promote, always recommended me for good jobs.

I'd planned on visiting Terrible Teddy, soon, and after speaking with McCullar, soon was now. I left McCullar's trailer, went over to G-3 Air, and hooked a helicopter ride from division to Eighteenth Airborne Corps' headquarters.

From the landing strip at Corps an MP Humvee took me over to Nicholson's hooch in the Corps' intelligence liaison section.

Nicholson was operating out of an M577 armored command vehicle with a sandbagged tent blossoming from the rear end of the track. An electrical generator beside the M577 pumped juice full blast, powering a Sears window-unit air conditioner propped on the back deck of the vehicle and blowing down into the tent. On a stake near the entrance someone had tacked a drawing of the Kool cigarette penguin, a hand-rolled smoke in its beak. Beneath the bird the words: "It's *très froid* inside."

I threw open the GP medium's front flap and said, "Ted?"

"Peter, my man. Enter and drop the flap."

Burly, smiling Ted Nicholson sat at a card table next to a French lieutenant-colonel. The French officer was a large man with a massive chest and heavy, bushy black eyebrows. The rear tent flap almost covered the entrance to the rear of the command vehicle, but I could see at least one other person was in the 577 sitting by the radio bank. Even with the generator running right outside I could hear the squawk of a radio.

As I took my helmet off and put it on an empty folding chair, Ted gave a fast introduction. "Lieutenant Colonel Antoine Mechain, Major Peter Ford." As I shook Mechain's hand the rear flap opened. Hollywood invasion — in uniform, only a French female officer would try that sultry glare. But the ploy didn't faze me, I recognized the gimmick. All female intel operatives have the smokey pout down pat. It's part of the arsenal, and this woman's struck me as second tier, a second-rate pout on a first-rate face. She was French all right, a French intelligence captain, a slim but athletic build, high waist, severely cut but bright brown hair with an auburn tone, deep brown eyes, a rakish burgundy beret tucked in her belt. As she watched me watch her, she rolled Chap Stick lip balm across her lips like the mentholated gook was haute couture lip gloss.

Her sultry act vanished. Mark of a pro, I thought, a quick read of the crowd. She came over to the table, extended her hand and said, "Captain Elise Neaves, sir."

I shook it. "You two the liaison team from Sixth Light?" I asked. France's Sixth Light Armored Division had screened the coalition ground offensive's deep left flank.

Mechain knit his eyebrows, glanced at Ted.

"They were," Ted said. "Now, they're just looking for a card game. What brings you to Corps, Pete?"

I didn't like the feel of Mechain and Neaves. Intelligence officers with Ted's background are in the business of knowing people everywhere and I knew Mechain and Neaves were part of that business. I'd played the game, too. Unlike me, Ted thoroughly enjoyed it. I wanted to gripe at Ted, about his loose lip on the Gunther subject. There was also the subject of the survivor of the village massacre. However, with the French team present, I canned that matter. But the murders—it might be interesting to get Mechain's and Neaves's reactions.

I sat down in a chair at the card table and started going over the incident at the river, speaking to Ted, not his guests. I kept it cool, said I knew he had some facts but he needed mine. I described what I'd witnessed, I mentioned Guyton's photos, I said the photos meant we could prosecute this war crime. If Mechain and Neaves knew Ted, they knew what I was getting at.

Then I gave Ted my theory. As I laid the theory out, Mechain and Neaves became intensely interested. It was such a plausible theory, neat, tied to known objectives.

"This doesn't take a lot of imagination, Ted. The man in the jumpsuit was looking for her, see? Consider the action as evidence. There's a time pressure here, a clock pushing the killer."

"He's not offing his mistress?" Mechain asked drily.

"Shit," I replied. I'd dealt with guys like Mechain. I gave the man a hot stare and said, evenly, "What if he is?"

"You make a good point," Mechain replied slickly.

Good. The lug picked up that I was in no mood for indifference.

Ted, reaching into his ice chest for a bottle of Evian water, said, "Pete . . . No one liked those orders." He nodded at me. I don't know what kind of answer he expected, so I didn't give him one.

Instead, Captain Neaves said to me, tartly, "Major, I am thoroughly puzzled. Why didn't you shoot and not say anything of it?"

Mechain grinned a toothy, square-toothed grin. He was amused at my silence, I suspect.

"What would you have done, Captain?" Ted asked.

"We'd have gone over and handled business," Neaves replied. "The hell with orders. Say you obey, keep the political cover story intact, do what you must do."

"So. Shoot back, kill the grotesque bastards, lie and cover up?" Ted asked.

Neaves nodded. "*Exactement.* Punish them and be done with it."

"Just another day on the Champs Elysee?"

"You can't put the Germans on an Indian reservation," Neaves snapped.

"You don't have the American press on your ass," Terrible Ted snapped back.

Neaves cocked an eyebrow. "It would have been better, Major Nicholson, if there had been live television cameras at the river. Quite possibly the surge of public resentment would have forced the politicians to respond."

Suddenly I got interested in Captain Neaves.

Ted grinned. "The political class wouldn't let us act, Elise. They had reasons. Consider the long-term

prospects in the Middle East. The Security Council only
authorized—"

"Ted—" I interrupted. Then I didn't know what to
say. I sat there, uncomfortable, aware that everyone was
uncomfortable, even the lout Mechain. Neaves stared at
me with those no-give brown eyes. Finally, I said, "Ted,
if you can break my theory, do it."

Ted went into a five-minute spiel, mocking what he
referred to as "Ford's theory of the crime," deriding my
explanation as a spy fiction concoction, then—slowly,
but getting there—after improvising, after adding his
own emphasis, he followed the lines of analysis I'd suggested to a logical conclusion. Ted, being a highly intel-
ligent man, listened to himself talk. As Ted talked and
went through it, as he listened to himself, Mechain
raised those massive black eyebrows, Neaves looked
pensive, her smooth forehead wrinkling. Finally, Ted
convinced himself that I might be very angry but I
wasn't nuts. The theory that we'd witnessed an Iraqi
bigwig committing a war crime piqued his interest and
appealed to his not-too-buried conscience.

"Okay," Ted finally said. "Pete, you're getting way
ahead of the system. Say the man is a Baath Party big
shot, Saddam still has to fall. There'll need to be a war
crimes commission."

"That's in the works, Ted. The disappeared Kuwaitis
and the environmental disaster. Look, you know the
people to push to get it started."

"And you don't?" Ted guffawed.

"The photos," I replied, ignoring his comment, "nail
the killers. This is an atrocity in the open, hard evidence, caught in the act."

Ted nodded, glanced at Mechain and Neaves, then

shrugged. "The photos. They enhanceable? Get me
copies of the photos and your After Action Report.
We'll look into it."

I stood, said good-bye to Mechain and Neaves, and
left.

I GOT A HELICOPTER FLIGHT BACK TO BATTALION. PFC
Guyton had already had the division's field photo lab
run three sets of prints of his photos. That evening Guy-
ton went with a courier on a run to division and Corps.
I had Guyton deliver the photos to Ted himself. I told
Guyton not to play poker with Major Nicholson because
Ted was a bad loser.

The next morning Ted called me on the field phone.
His cynicism had dissipated and he sounded like the
good soldier he was. "You've something here, with old
Jumpsuit," Ted said. *Jumpsuit.* How'd I miss that
stroke? A smart quip and Ted names the killer. "I had the
photos enhanced. Now, this is interesting and it adds a
neat twist to your theory of the crime. Jumpsuit's wearing a wig, Peter, the big curls are fake." What about his
mustache, I asked. "That might be real. Can't go that far
with the enhancement. The pixels fuzz." Ted said that
this didn't have the make of an ordinary atrocity. Christ,
I interrupted, Ted, what is an *ordinary* atrocity? Ted
went, aw shit, lighten up, you're too worked up. Chill
out, Ted said, and don't get married to a guess. Frickin'
photos don't tell you everything. That's why spy satellites ain't replaced spies. "I mean," Ted boomed, "you
don't know what you saw, do you? And you saw it . . .
Lemme speak to a coupla guys who know God. State's

making Saddam a criminal case. This'll tickle 'em . . .
You cool now?"

"I'm holding my breath."

"Better your breath than your balls."

"I need another favor."

"Go."

"Can you, or somebody, check on a young man our
battalion picked up at the river? We sent him to
Dhahran." I gave Ted the background. Abdul, that was
the kid's name, who crossed the river with his friends in
the raft, the teen with the Babylonian figs and swimmer's build. The short version: Abdul escaped the village massacre. He reached our battalion the night after
the Iraqis smashed his town, covered in rancid mud,
scared but too angry to show it. A sergeant brought him
to me and said, "His family's over there, dead on the
riverbank." The kid tried to tough it, at first snapping to
attention like a drill field troop, but that act didn't last.
He started sobbing.

We fed him, the medics washed him down with a
hose, put clean clothes on him. In clean clothes Abdul
went back to tough. He pointed to the parachute jump
wings on my uniform. "What's it like to leap from a
plane and fall a thousand meters?" he asked. I told him
you trained to handle it. The magic words, *training* and
discipline, reduce your risk.

Abdul bunked with the medics. The next day, as the
battalion prepared to withdraw to the south, I saw
Abdul, brown T-shirt, scrounged boots, staring across
the water. I looked across the river, at the village. Christ,
forgive us. The engine on the medic track coughed,
kicked on. I told Abdul to climb in and move out of
here. The kid had to quit looking at the smoke. That

night, during a halt in the road march, I saw Abdul talking with the battalion intelligence officer. The next day the intel section shipped him to the Red Crescent office in Dhahran.

"Dhahran, Red Cross-Red Crescent. I heard back on your Shiite boy," Ted Nicholson told me a couple of days after I asked him to look in on Abdul. "They said he signed out a week ago with a Saudi Army officer and an American Green Beret."

THE DAY BEFORE OUR BATTALION FLEW BACK TO THE States (we returned via Dhahran International), an intel officer from Central Command showed up at headquarters. We sat in her Humvee and she conducted a debrief on the massacre. She introduced herself as Captain Marta Martinez.

Captain Martinez was an all-business brunette, dark, flashing Spanish eyes and sharp Aztec cheekbones. Despite her baggy desert BDUs, my brain easily imagined perfect legs. Martinez showed me a couple of enhanced photos in the file on her lap, black-and-white glossies that caught Jumpsuit in profile. I put my finger on his face, asked her if she had any leads on the man. She shook her head. What about the victims, the old men and, in particular, the nurse? "Nada," she replied.

After our triumphal return to the States, Ted Nicholson got promoted to lieutenant colonel and DA assigned him to an intel slot at European Command. He dropped me a letter about his promotion and new assignment. He added this PS: "Jumpsuit's lost in the shuffle, I'm afraid, but trust I'll keep a recce eye out. Attention, now. The abstract: we speculate all fricking day on possible combinations in the card deck. The concrete: that's our real job, to KNOW the deal out there, which means BE out there, in it. I don't know the deal with the murder you witnessed and, pal, you don't either. Don't get married to a guess. We're on the bloody third stone, I do know that, and the bitch eats shoe leather. OK? If anything pops, I'll clue you."

I read that PS and thought, Nicholson, you bum. For God's sake, I saw a murder, not a deck of cards.

CHAPTER 4

THAT LAST YEAR IN THE ARMY—I GOT SICK, THE KIND of sickness that sneaks up and nicks you, drains you a little at a time.

I left the tank battalion for a job in Washington, a slot in Clarendon supporting military attachés serving in European Command. It was a good high-viz job. Ted phoned me the day after I reported for duty and said he knew I'd do my damnedest to protect the uniforms from being the fall guys for the spies and diplomats.

Since he was back in European Command headquarters, Ted and I talked, frequently. I didn't figure it out, but from the far side of the Atlantic, Ted determined that something was akilter. "You don't sound like yourself, Pete," Ted said one Friday morning at my desk in Clarendon but afternoon where he sat in the bunker in Stuttgart. I told him I had office disease, bad lightbulbs in the white ceiling fixtures, gray metal desks, puke-green walls.

But I was wrong. Perhaps I was suffering from a chronic fatigue virus, a gritty little systemic bug. Maybe I had my own sapping little Gulf War syndrome, the unidentifiable pestilence. My energy level plunged. My ability to stiff the manipulative demands of spies and diplomats decreased. The bottom line was I didn't do the job.

I ran into Ambassador Everett Kilean at a State Department function held at George Washington University. He asked me why I hadn't told him I'd landed in Washington. He wasn't stupid, he knew I still blamed him. What the old man wanted to know was if I still hated him, but he lacked the guts to ask. I told him I'd been swamped at my job, and that I was ill. For the length of time it took him to sip a double Chivas on the rocks, that Ivy League conniver persuasively portrayed a fretting gray-haired aristocrat. When I wouldn't elaborate on my illness, when I turned down a lunch invite, Kilean brought up the After Action Report McCullar sent him. I've got to give him credit. Kilean didn't go near the murder of the nurse. He said, softly and convincingly, that he knew it had to be double tough for me to sit there and watch that. He'd sent a copy of my report to a new war crimes section at State and another to a friend of his at the United Nations. He said it was a long shot but you had to take those long shots. He introduced me to a couple of staffers on the intelligence oversight committee. I left after that. I told Kilean I felt tired.

Kilean's secretary called me the next day. He came on the line and told me he could recommend an excellent internist, a woman, great diagnostician. Kilean said, with a cool urgency, "Let me call Dr. Savka on your behalf, get you through her backlog." I wrote her name down, said I'd let him know.

I never saw Kilean's doctor. The next week I went to Walter Reed, had the clinic do a complete physical. The Army doctors said I was a screaming stud, nothing wrong. The mononucleosis test was negative. Epstein-Barr was negative. CMV negative. I was impressively perfecto, gymnast lean and fat free.

A month later I saw a psychologist who diagnosed a mild clinical depression. She'd seen a lot of depression, lately, she said with a nod, other patients in their late twenties or early thirties. "Reason with me," she said as I lay on the couch staring at the yellow acoustic tile on her office ceiling. "The war, Major Ford, for you and many others, it produced an acute, intense response." I glanced at her out of the corner of my eye. She peered at me over her bifocals, eyes saucering in the gold frames. "How do you return to the farm after you've seen Paris? That's the World War One parallel. I realize the Arabian desert isn't Paris, but, perhaps for people like you . . . ?"

She perked when we made direct eye contact. "Am I close, now?" she asked. "I know these are difficult thoughts, difficult to express, and often it's difficult for a man to put difficult feelings into words, but there's truth here, in this idea, isn't there? I'm not pressing for your answer, I want you to sit with it, consider it. Now, the military's on a diet. What's the word I'm after? Cutting back, cutting back on soldiers. Though you've a successful career, you and many others, you're not alone in this, you may feel discarded. This magnifies the emotional depletion you feel in the aftermath of your war. Are we connecting?" She smiled, nodded, waiting for my nod.

Instead I told her about the village and the river and the murders. I told her how we sat there, paralytic. My face flushed. I could taste the peroxide, saliva on my tongue burning like peroxide. You want the truth? I asked her. I'm ready to kill that fucker, to clean my goddamn brain out.

The psychologist's bifocals slipped down her aquiline nose. Her legs crossed, tightly, calf on shin with the sheen of stretching nylon. She didn't reply. She was pro enough to know at times she's paid to listen.

THAT SPRING—1992—I STARTED FEELING STRONG again, until a bad flu nailed me for three weeks. That flu virus wouldn't die. The bug stuck so deep I began to think it'd take chemo to kill it. When I returned to the office a small seismic shift had occurred. Someone else had my desk. They offered the attaché job at the embassy in Mauritania. I had requested assignment to Greece, Turkey, Kenya, or anywhere in the Middle East. Mauritania? Decisions get made, Officer Personnel Management told me. Despite my special skills and military-diplomatic experience, my future was Mauritania.

That same month the Army introduced a program that made resigning attractive. If you'd put in at least ten years you'd receive a lump sum or an annual stipend. In May I had ten.

I resigned, took the lump.

I'd promised Dr. Gunther I'd tell him if I quit the Army, so I wrote him a letter, through his headquarters in Brussels. Then I slept for a month. I only left the apartment to buy milk, bread, and Vitamin C. Everyone who's been in that kind of funk knows the cycle. Anger, fatigue, resentment, a loop of perpetual vultures.

One morning the phone rang and it wasn't a telemarketer. It was Dr. Gunther, live via satellite phone from a Hospital for Humanity field clinic on the Thai-Burmese border. The clinic had wounded Karen refugees who'd fled the Burmese Army's latest genocidal attack. If you haven't heard of the Karen, don't sweat it, like most oppressed people they bleed and die off-camera. Gunther gave me his pitch, with his usual sharp wit. He needed experienced security personnel who understood the pressures on Non-Governmental Organizations, people who knew how to work with nutty do-gooders and hostile zealots, men who could facilitate understandings with fascist bureaucrats and brute warlords and stupid punks.

I told Gunther the thought of security work in hell-holes made me puke. I said on the days I managed to shave I'd thought about going back to graduate school. I admitted, since I no longer had a job, that I had an interest in making money and a business degree looked like money.

"Then go do it," Gunther said through the crackling orbital static. "*Pliss*—off your rear."

I told him I thought it was too late for this year, too late to apply to any decent MBA program.

Gunther ripped out a complex paragraph of curses and instructions, in a language I identified as French, German, and possibly Swahili. He finished with "You go out of bed, Peter. I'll get you into a school."

Three days later I received express mail letters from

Harvard Business School and from Thunderbird out in Tucson.

Damn. Look what a Nobel Prize unlocks.

Damn.

That afternoon I went to the gym.

I SPENT THE NEXT TWO YEARS IN BOSTON, GETTING an MBA.

In the spring of 1994 R. B. Guyton phoned from Boston Logan. He had a layover on a flight to Europe, Bosnia via London and Aviano, Italy. Guyton said he hadn't reenlisted, but the Army'd been good. He'd slapped twenty thousand in his college account, through the GI education program, and another thirty grand in his checking account through his GI poker program. Guyton said he was heading for Bosnia on a photo assignment, a freelance gig with *Newsweek.* Desert Storm had launched his photographic career, the tank photos, the hundreds of pix of soldiers. When he showed his portfolio to *Newsweek*'s photo editor in August 1992, she'd flipped. And speaking of photos, "Your friend, Colonel Nicholson? Called me a month ago, wanted new copies of *the* photos, the murders? You still wanta whack that Jumpsuit, Major, go postal and *whack* the guy? I ran Nicholson a set and I *ast* about you, where you're at. He said to say hello and tell you he's still pissed off at you."

"Did . . . did Nicholson say why he wanted photos?"

"No. I *ast* him, but, mind games, y'know. I didn't get nothing. . . . They're callin' my flight. You gettin' a bizness degree, huh? Have a line on a job?"

I told him I'd interviewed with a couple of New York investment firms.

"Big money," Guyton whistled.

NO ONE ENTIRELY RATIONAL COULD BE BITTER AFTER walking away with three point eight million—but I'm getting ahead of myself.

The MBA and my foreign languages got me hired at Herald-Acre International Investments. The letter of personal recommendation from Ambassador Kilean also helped. By the fall of 1995 Herald's principals had me running their New York-based Middle Eastern client section, which consisted of me and Samir Aflaq, a forty-one-year-old Syrian émigré with a small black mustache, soft eyes, and very delicate hands. Samir was a gay, Greek Orthodox Arab Christian with a photographic memory for numbers and a talent for finding unusual, lucrative corporate bonds. I was Samir's boss in name only. Samir said he never wanted to run anything except the numbers, thank you, so please, he told our boss, Dr. Barbara Glassman, you have Peter manage our section. Samir was discreet to a fault, as discreet as he was tidy. The man organized his paper clips. My first Samir theory didn't take a lot of stretch. With his contacts in Singapore and the Caymans, Samir was well positioned to bust UN sanctions and invest laundered funds—perhaps Iraqi funds. But there was no evidence, only my ingrained and unfair suspicion. During that first year at Herald I developed other theories about Samir, and kept them to myself. But he had the make, like my dad used to say. When we'd go to lunch at a chop house Samir liked, he'd cross himself in the Orthodox manner, then fold his fingers together and say grace. One afternoon he told me his younger brother was a priest. His older brother was a businessman, a classic Levantine merchant, Samir called him, who'd fled the Syrian regime but was a "bad sort." Another afternoon he came into my office and told me his father had been a scholar and had translated five books of the New Testament into English from a Syriac codex that no one in Rome even knew existed. A week later, in the chop house, he told me his father, before the old man died, had disowned him. He said his father had told him that he wished Samir had never existed. He said his older brother in Istanbul never spoke to him. "Do you see why I didn't become a mathematics professor?" Samir asked. I didn't tell Samir that he'd never mentioned a desire to be a mathematics professor. The Buddha said desire is suffering, so I just listened and nodded. Did he have the make, this complex man? Deep cover twists identity. The best intelligence agents are such good con men they border on the sociopathic, they know how to get your frequency, to pluck your strings, flatter and evade.

In June of 1997 I met Trish at a party up in Tarrytown. She wore purple eye shadow and had three diamond rings, one on her right pinkie. She drank vodka martinis and loathed peanuts. When she smiled, dimples sweetened her face. She said she'd tried to run an art gallery in Soho but now she worked at a start-up investment operation in midtown Manhattan. The hardest part of her transition from Soho to midtown was deleting the word "fuck" from her casual conversation. She ran one of her long fingers across the nape of my neck.

We started seeing each other. One evening, in January 1998, Trish and I were having dinner in my apartment, and the phone rings and its Dr. Gunther, calling from Brussels. Had I heard about the NGO conference in Aruba? No? If you're interested, Peter, in possibly managing investment portfolios for some of these organizations, perhaps you should attend. He gave me the details and said he'd be there for at least one afternoon session. I thanked him, said I'd consider it. If I didn't make it to Aruba we agreed to get together next time he came through New York.

When I described Gunther's proposal to Trish, she said if I didn't go I was a fool — cute, but a fool. No, she couldn't come with me, though that was a delightful invitation. She had a new project out in Silicon Valley, one that was approaching either splashy IPO or ignominious collapse. I said that was the first I'd heard of her trip out to San Jose. She shrugged, it'd come up yesterday, she replied, and my head's spinning, Pete. Pour me another glass of the Pomerol, and tell me everything there is to know about a global *icon* like Dr. Gunther. What I don't know about you Ford simply *amazes* me.

CHAPTER 5

AT THE OFFICE THE NEXT DAY, AFTER I MENTIONED Gunther's phone call and after I went into a spiel about how financially iffy NGOs can be, Samir said, "Your hesitancy disturbs me. You must go to this in Aruba, for contacts, Peter, for future *entrée*." Twenty minutes later Samir met Barbara tête-à-tête in the hallway. *Après* Samir, big blonde Barbara Glassman walked by my office and crooked her finger. In her mega-office, a museum of Victorian knickknacks and baroque figurines, Barbara asked me why on Earth I seemed reluctant to explore an opportunity. Look, I said, Barb, this isn't personal, it's professional. Most of the big NGOs are already financially wired, and the small ones won't generate the business you expect. Don't assume what I expect, Pete, Barbara replied. Think PR. A link with a solid aid organization is fabulous PR.

I FLEW TO ARUBA. I SPENT THE FIRST DAY HANGING out, watching, identifying zealots and pragmatists, hustlers and healers. Mrs. Urestes was there, representing the International Committee of the Red Cross. I kissed her on the cheek, she squeezed my hand hard, and I could feel the bones in her strong nurse's fingers. The morning of the second day I attended a seminar run by something called the Core Value Coalition International. I'm not sure why I went. I figured it for a Christian medical group of some type, political left or right, but no—a bad guess—the CVC International was a hustle, featuring a forty-minute harangue for the cameras by a Dr. Eliot Chew from Los Angeles, California. I know the international aid community. It's a religious order, even for the most secular and agnostic activists. The best people and organizations in the community have few peers in terms of decency and commitment, but, like in every religion, you get the cults and fakes. It took me about six seconds to peg Chew as a fake, not for his policies, but for his pitch and his TV preacher eyes. Chew began by demanding that the governments of Zimbabwe, Botswana, and Namibia end their limited elephant tusk and ivory sales and that the 1989 complete moratorium on trade in ivory be reinstituted immediately. Okay, that's a hot topic, one with room for legitimate disagreement. Elephant poaching is a big problem in game preserves throughout sub-Saharan Africa, and to an extent the lure of ivory sales encourages the poaching. But the subject is also a hot button for organizations more interested in attracting attention and raising funds than stopping poaching. Save the elephants, send us money. A woman from Save Wild Africa, a very legit antipoaching group I'd worked with

in Kenya, and one that does save the elephants, asked
Chew if he realized there was a place for indigenous
people to sell limited amounts of elephant ivory, that
these sales put cash in conservation trusts. Chew didn't
debate her point. He attacked her for "kowtowing to
globalist market fascism." I raised my hand and asked
Dr. Chew if he'd ever been to Africa, say, out with the
Masai and their cattle? No, he replied, but his data col-
lectors had. And with whom, he asked, are *you* associ-
ated?

"Hospital for Humanity," I replied. Shit, I thought,
let someone try and dispute that.

DR. GUNTHER BLEW IN JUST BEFORE NOON. I MET
him right after his quickie press conference. My mother
had said Gunther was an old man at thirty, those hard
years in Africa and Southeast Asia and the recurrent
malaria cutting deep lines into his tanned, round face.
The Gunther I remembered as a child had seemed so an-
cient, so bald. But now, with his vigor, dominating
stamina, and regular regimen of testosterone injections,
you had trouble believing that he was seventy-eight.
The early graying and the balding had stopped, his bald
top surrounded by brown and gray locks that circled the
slick zone and crept down his neck to finish in a short
ponytail.

"A ponytail?"

"A recent affectation, Peter. So, *pliss,* how goes it?"

"I'm making money," I replied.

He spent all of five hours at the conference. After his
speech to the press he had a sandwich, took a half hour
to freshen up, then spent his next three hours chairing a

discussion on cooperative fund-raising. He introduced me at that meeting. He mentioned my mother, said I was now a financial consultant.

The last hour he spent with me in my hotel room.

We sat on the metal chairs on the small balcony overlooking the street. He insisted he had to watch for the airport limo. I asked him if he ever turned off his cell phone and he grinned. He liked the view from the balcony, of the boulevard, of the long pier, the docks, the blue water in the harbor with the sailing ships. Do you have field glasses, Peter, to look at the ships?

No, I said, no field glasses. I no longer need them.

Room service arrived and the young woman brought out a silver tray with a pot of oolong. He drank two cups, asked about New York, my job, then started talking about a new project in Africa (he didn't mention the country but I got the impression it was Burundi), and the big, messy war in the Congo.

Then suddenly he asked, "I meant to ask you earlier, how does your job fit you?"

"My job?"

He nodded.

"I like the pace," I replied. "Fast, decisive. You either do it or you get run over."

His gray-blue eyes, behind the lenses of his glasses, magnified. I knew he was thinking about my mother. That made me think about Mom, her death, and, so help me, the murder of that other nurse across the Euphrates.

LATER THAT EVENING, AN HOUR OR SO AFTER DR. Gunther left for the airport, I walked over to the harbor, to take a closer look at the ships. I noticed a woman standing on the long pier, the white one near the marina at the end of the boulevard. The lady wore a red, flowered dress, a hibiscus pattern that didn't hide her wasp waist, a pair of dark black sunglasses, and a wide-brimmed hat with a red silk ribbon. Her red-brown hair fell on her shoulders.

First glance and I wasn't sure, so I hesitated. You're mistaken, man, I thought. So I walked over to the railing on the marina side of the pier, got another angle. Yes, it's either her or a dead ringer. Pin the hair up, put her in fatigues and that's Elise Neaves, French Army intelligence. Her incisive comment about the possible effect of live TV during the atrocities—I'd never forgotten it.

Then I noticed Neaves was standing near another woman. The other woman was a little taller than Elise, perhaps five five, plain brown hair in a bun. Like Elise, the woman wore sunglasses, except hers were the broad aviator model with deep green lenses. This lady had a sharp nose and very taut, athletic angles to her tanned face. She wore gray slacks and a simple, forgettable brown blouse. A black plastic cell phone case dangled from a leather loop on her belt. Diminutive yet rugged—this other woman had the possible make of a doctor or surgical nurse, I thought, the tough field type, except there was an edge to her that didn't quite fit the medical professional. So what bugs me? I asked myself. Plain brown hair, simple clothing, her lack of distinction, her detachment. I tell you, she didn't look like anybody's sister.

I hesitated again, a hesitation based on habits four years hadn't thoroughly dulled. Elise and the woman didn't seem to be talking to each other, but they were together, in the way two people arrive at an embassy party expecting to meet. Total pros can hide it, unless they think they've no need to hide. This duet on the pier had that planned collision feel.

Elise turned, cast one of those panoramic glances down the boulevard. Did she notice me?

Action—the other woman turned, walked off, casting the briefest discreet glance in my direction, a discreet glance in every direction but the harbor's. If Neaves was a French military intelligence officer, you had to figure this gal for a player.

I waited, then Elise turned on her pump and walked in the other direction.

My curiosity hit about a ninety-three on a hundred scale. Watch one, watch the other, catch up and speak to Neaves or stand pat and try and figure out why they met here on the pier. Sex and suspicion, Pete, what the hell more could you want to pass ten minutes of time?

As Neaves walked from the pier to the boulevard I critiqued my assumptions. Man, you're operating on sensation and buzz, I thought. What if they came to the dock together and I missed it? Is this any of my business? But I remembered my old man's line, "Certain kinds of events attract familiar faces." I wanted to speak to Neaves, but the mood of the encounter I'd witnessed on the pier—no, I couldn't shake that sensation and buzz.

Neaves disappeared in the crowd, heading back to hotel row and the main drag. I walked along the edge of the dock. Nothing tied up down below, no boat. To the left, fifteen meters, was a walkway leading to the motorboats and motor yacht marina. To the right, twenty meters away, a small rock shelf, a little boy with a stick

poking at a shell. Directly out in the harbor, five an-
chored sailing yachts, one a big sloop, and farther out a
rusting coastal freighter that looked intensely red and
yellow in the sunlight. I checked my watch. Six-sixteen
P.M. local. I scanned the dock, the marina, the road leading out to the jetty. The discreet lady with the edge had
disappeared. Okay, Neaves. I turned and headed toward
the center of town.

THE HIBISCUS DRESS HAD THE HOT SHINE OF A RED
flare, like hey, here I am, forget the crowd. I saw her
enter a small hotel named the Orion. There was a bar
across the street, several bars, actually. I went into the
one with the big bay window facing the Orion's entrance. I ordered a Guiness, took a seat. You couldn't
see into the hotel, the awnings and dark panes obscured
everything but the open front door. Fifteen minutes of
sipping drained the half-pint of stout. An empty glass in
front of me and I still hadn't decided on what to do,
other than say hello, and attempt to satisfy my bout of
intense counterintelligence curiosity. Maybe she was on
vacation. Though French intel was notorious for using
and co-opting aid agencies, whatever squirrelly conspiracy Neaves may or may not be engineering wasn't my
business, not anymore. I began to convince myself to
forget it, let it fade.

No sunglasses now—Neaves walked out of the
Orion. I stood and left the bar.

Just before she reached the curb I said, "Captain
Neaves? Aren't you Elise Neaves?"

She whirled, startled, very nonpro.

"I didn't mean to startle you. Pete Ford." I stuck my

hand out. "Didn't we meet in Saudi? Weren't you in the French Army?" I repeated what I said in French. *"On s'est vu en Arabie, n'est-ce pas? Vous etiez a ce moment dans l'armée française . . ."*

She blinked her brown eyes, eyes magnified by mascara, and said, "I had no idea you spoke such French, Major Ford. Or is it colonel now?"

"It's mister. I got out."

"Oh." An eyebrow arched.

"What about you? What brings you to Aruba?"

"Holiday . . . You, also?"

"I'm attending the NGO conference. I'm . . . sure you know about it."

"So . . . you work for an aid agency, now?"

"Investments, I'm with an investment firm. We're after endowment work. . . . Are you on your way to dinner?"

"Are you asking me to dinner?"

"Yes."

"Then we're on our way to dinner."

OVER A DINNER OF FRESH SWORDFISH SHE TOLD ME she was no longer in the military, that she'd been a reservist, anyway, and now she worked for a small software company in Lyons. Elise lied very well.

We went to a calypso joint. We had a rum punch. She danced very well.

We walked back to her hotel. I told her I was leaving the next day, late in the afternoon. She said she had a flight out the next evening. I tried to steer the conversation—to her good looks, to sex, I had lost all interest in her rendezvous with the woman at the pier—but pivotal topics like the weather, the NGO conference, and her desire to have one of my Herald-Acre International cards for her file intervened. As for her card and her software firm? She didn't have one with her, not on vacation. Yes, Elise could weave and dodge with plausible deniability. She knew I wanted to make a pass at her. Exotic Caribbean island, chance encounter, delightful evening, the hormones pump. That's how she read the moment, read me, and that was an accurate read. But I could tell, just flat tell Elise was still on duty.

We kissed good night in front of the Orion, my hand on her neck. Her lips burned. We talked about doing a little shopping the next morning, and left it at that.

I AWOKE, LOOKED AT THE CEILING, HEARD RAINDROPS striking the balcony window. I listened to the rain for four or five minutes, listened to it slack off. A brief tropical gust. I glanced at my watch—two-seventeen A.M. local—thought about flipping on the television for a weather report but decided I preferred the slow drip sound of the rain.

I had absolutely no reason to get up, but I couldn't sleep, either. I lay there, wide awake. I thought about Elise, thought about Trish and San Jose. Maybe I should call Trish out in California, if she was still in California. I considered ringing her apartment in New York. No, forget that, I'll call her when I get back. For sure.

I got out of bed, pulled on a shirt and pants. I went to the balcony door, opened it, felt the burst of wet, cool air and the darkness. The rain had almost stopped so I stepped out on the balcony. The neon signs on the stores and clubs were dark and dead, the exception a noxious blue and green neon parrot flickering above a shuttered café. I gripped the wrought iron trellis, smelled the potted violets in the box on the ledge. The violets were wet. I leaned over the ledge, took a deep breath, got a lung full of the lush, heavy, tropic air.

And I saw a flash out in the harbor. No, I didn't get it. The flash was flarelike, a narrow yellow burst of light and fire that erupted, dimmed quickly. I peered out into the harbor, at the beaded chains of lights on the yachts.

Then the fire leaped, a rising string of sparks and a sudden constellation of flame. Fire in a yacht's rigging? Is that what I see?

I knew what I had to do and I had to do it quickly. I left the balcony, blew right through my room and raced downstairs to the desk clerk. "I think a ship's on fire," I said, "in the harbor."

The clerk blinked a pair of sleepy, big eyes, moved a dred off his forehead. I saw the bong on the registration counter. Shit. Forget him. Out the door into the street, I ran barefoot for the pier, slapped by one, two, several pellets of rain.

No doubt now. One of the big yachts, the big sloop out in the harbor, was burning, an orange tongue of fire licking the mast, a hot glow at the stern.

I reached the pier above the rock shelf. So much so fast—I cupped my hands and shouted out into the harbor. Then I heard her. A woman in a dingy beside the sloop was screaming, "OhmyGod ohmyGod, they're on board." She raised a paddle, I saw her in silhouette, and suddenly she tipped and fell out of the dingy into the harbor.

I slid down the seawall and dived. It was sixty meters

out there, and the water had a storm chop to it, but I made it quick.

Her wet hair streaked her face and forehead and she was clinging to the dingy. "Were you on board? How many on board?"

"Her—his children. Gawd."

I saw faces up on the deck, peering down, I heard their frightened yells. I clambered up the ladder onto the boat and into a sudden wall of black smoke. You could feel the heat creep in the smoke.

"Here, we're here." The woman gave me a little girl's hand as she balanced and started to drop another child down to the dingy. A man stood beside me, coughing into his fist.

"You okay?"

The man's coughing fit continued.

"Lasko. Give me Lasko," the woman said coolly.

I passed the little girl to the woman.

The man pushed past me.

"Jersey. OhmyGod where's Jersey?"

"Ellen—"

"Where?" I asked.

The man, bald and with a gut, coughed hard, got out the word "woman" and pointed.

"Below deck?"

"Second door. Right side."

I ripped off my soaked T-shirt and put it to my nose and mouth. The smoke broke enough and there was light from the fire on the deck and the stern. I ducked into the passageway, wishing to God I had a flashlight. I used my hand, felt one door, the second, shoved it open. No electricity, no light, wall of heat raking my face, but my naked foot stepped on her body. Coughing now, breathing smoke and wet shirt, I tried to pick the woman up from the floor, lost her, so I dragged her, dragged her straight through a sheet of smoke and onto the deck.

I threw her over my shoulders, dodged a crate or something, maneuvered through the smoke and reached the side of the sloop.

No dingy down there, the shape of the dingy moving away in the firelit darkness. *I hadn't been away a minute.*

"We thought you'd died," the man yelled.

Good Lord, I thought.

I balanced the woman, stood up on the side, and jumped. We both smacked hard on the water, and when I came up and brought her up to the air, I couldn't tell if she was breathing.

The dingy engine was sputtering on, the boat swinging wildly.

Man, that bastard. At least he's coming back.

I dragged the woman's head up, laid her body on my hip, started a sidestroke. "Here, damn you," I yelled.

The dingy bow just missed my head. Four arms appeared, grabbed the woman and brought her up. "Start mouth to mouth," I said. But no one started mouth to mouth until I came over the side. "You're going to sink us," the man yelled, or maybe it was one of the women in the dingy. Some gutless jackass yelled it.

"Shut up," I replied as I put my thumb on the mouth of Jersey and cleared her air passage, starting the mouth to mouth. A half-dozen breaths and she puked. Good sign. I wiped out her mouth with my fingers. The dingy was moving now, toward shore, moving awkwardly, three women, two children, the man on board, me half in and half out. Smoke blanketed the water, no sign of flames but the clinging, heavy, carbon smoke smothering you. I gave Jersey another breath, tried to raise my legs so I didn't cause so much resistance on the water. I noticed there was at least one fire engine on the wharf and another boat approaching, an emergency craft of some sort. I gave Jersey another dozen, slow breaths.

"We thought you were dead," the man said again.

I didn't reply to the jerk. As we neared the strand, three men lowered themselves from the dock, started shouting and signaling. Two searchlights flicked on. I started coughing again, suddenly aware of a burn on my arm, aware of the sound of police sirens. A searchlight beam fixed on me, on Jersey, her dark red hair on her naked shoulders, the red lump on her forehead. With a flutter her eyes opened, and she coughed, coughed harshly. I felt the rock ledge under my feet so I slipped off the boat, stood, put my hand on her back. "Lean forward," I said. "Keep coughing."

As she leaned forward, I saw blood on the back of her head.

"Was there an explosion?" I asked.

She looked at me, her eyes starry and distant, then she coughed again. Now four men were around us, dragging the dingy to the rock shelf, three men picking up Jersey, lifting her, passing her to other hands on the pier, carrying her toward an emergency van.

"Help, mon?"

A big hand pulled me up on the pier. I tried but couldn't stand. I slumped forward, dropped to my knees, then put my head over the side, over the water.

The smoke did it. I could feel the heavy, wet, stinking smoke in my lungs and my gut. That's why I puked.

THREE A.M. TO FIVE A.M.: I SPENT THOSE HOURS AT police headquarters. The cops brought me ice water, let me have several whiffs of oxygen from a resuscitation tank. I told my story five times. The police hauled in two other witnesses, rumheads sucking black coffee. Yeah, they had the basic details. They'd noticed a fire in the harbor, on a yacht, and though half-drunk they'd run down the pier yelling for the fire department. The chief inspector took me into his office, told me he suspected a galley fire started it, an on-board propane explosion, he nodded, an unfortunate incident.

I CRAWLED OUT OF BED AROUND ONE P.M. THAT'S when I discovered the name of the sloop. She was the *Peace Warrior,* owned by television producer Josiah Bridger and the international ecological action organization, *EcoClash!* Both CNN International and Fox were running video clips of the damaged ship. The TV reports blamed it on an accidental galley fire. One woman had serious smoke inhalation injuries, the Australian actress Jersey Rampling. Ms. Rampling had been flown to Miami that morning. No mention of me, though CNN's anchor said Bridger was going to hold a news conference in Aruba. They flashed a picture of Bridger. Yes, he was the jerk who left me on board with Jersey.

I thought about Elise. I shaved quickly, dressed, jogged down the stairs and street to the Hotel Orion. I

asked for her at the desk. No, no Neaves registered. I
asked if she'd checked out. No, no Neaves at this hotel
last night. I described Elise. Oh, yes, her, Room 211.
She did check out. But was her name Neaves? Yes, I
said, I've known her for several years. What name did
she register under? I cannot give you that information,
the clerk replied. Not for ten dollars? I asked.

When I put the bill in his hand, the clerk struck a key
on his computer. "Margarete Erica Schmidt, Freiburg,
Germany."

BACK AT THE CONFERENCE HOTEL I TRIED TO FIND
Josiah Bridger but his people shook their heads, waved
me off. When I explained what I'd done the night before, his aides said they knew nothing about my in-
volvement. At the moment Mr. Bridger was huddling
with several fellow *EcoClash!* coordinators. The meeting could not be interrupted.

I went to the police station. The chief inspector gave
me Jersey Rampling's address in Sydney, Australia.
"The yacht owner thank you for what you did?" the
chief inspector asked. When I told him no, he grinned.
"He's big. Don't sound good, huh? He left you and the
woe-mun on board. Nope, Not good."

I left the police station and went to my hotel. By then
it was a hustle to get to the airport to catch my flight to
New York.

I RETURNED TO WORK THE NEXT DAY. ABOUT FOUR
that afternoon I flipped on the TV set in my office.
Bridger was finally holding his news conference.

Bridger claimed the fire on his ship had gravely damaged the cause of creating a nuclear-free world. After Aruba, the *Peace Warrior*'s next scheduled stop was the French space launch facility in French Guiana, off South America. the *Peace Warrior*'s crew had planned to protest the launch of a nuclear-powered communications satellite France was lofting on behalf of a consortium of North American and European corporations.

The smile on my face felt cold.

Damn, I thought. Elise Neaves and her friend on the pier. Now I've got one hell of a theory.

CHAPTER 6

I DIDN'T HAVE MUCH TIME TO THEORIZE ON ELISE
and the *Peace Warrior*.

The next day Barbara Glassman had her fatal heart
attack.

Samir found her in her office, gasping. When he
yelled I ran down the hallway. Everyone else on the
floor ran, too. Fran the receptionist kept her head and
called EMS.

Barbara was dead by the time EMS showed up.

I couldn't bother with Elise Neaves. Barbara's death
was tragic and the beginning of Herald's downward spi-
ral. For the next six months the Western European and
the East Asian section chiefs took turns failing at Barbara's job.

But I didn't forget about the *Peace Warrior* affair entirely. I wrote Jersey Rampling a letter and in May 1998
I got a large envelope back from Sydney. Rampling re-

membered me, she remembered the moment when she
snapped out of it and I told her to lean forward. Her
friend Ellen had filled in the details, including the one
about Bridger moving the dingy away from the sloop.
As for my question about how she hit her head, she hon-
estly didn't remember. A total blank. She thought she'd
been out on the deck, not in her cabin. Whatever—the
recurrent headaches were awful. She thanked me for
saving her life, said if I was in Sydney to give her a call,
said if she made it to New York she'd call me. The envelope included an autographed eight-by-twelve color
glossy of Jersey Rampling filling out a bikini. In the
photo she was a knockout. In the dark in the water she'd
looked wretched.

WHEN BARBARA DIED WE LOST OUR LEADER. WE
floundered, ended up in an extensive internal audit that
consumed my time. Trish got absorbed in another California deal, something large with tentacles. She started
pouring all of her own money into a project out in San
Jose. "Internet start-up," she said. She no longer wore
purple eye shadow or a diamond on her pinkie. In fact,
she had no diamonds. Late that fall she sold her Green-
wich Village apartment for cash.

In early 1999 Trish moved in with me. Yes, we were
more or less living together. More at first, to my delight,
then less and less. May, April, I didn't see much of her.
When she wasn't traveling she was at the gym, sweating. Trish became so thin and taut from aerobic exercise
her dimples shrank to hard lines.

In late June she moved to San Jose. In July she
called, frantic. A deal with the venture capitalists from

San Francisco had failed. She needed investors, pronto. I helped her, did it for her because I would do anything for her. I pushed some of my parents' old personal contacts, even Ambassador Kilean. Trish said she felt like I did too much—she was only able to pay me with winks and promises. I said I didn't need to be paid.

Out in San Jose, one Sunday afternoon in August 1999, Trish created MercMerge. In San Jose, about that same time, she met Lloyd. I didn't hear much about Lloyd, other than he had expertise in precious metal futures.

Trish asked me for advice on corporate structure, but that was after she'd met Lloyd and after our relationship had lost its structure.

HOW COULD ANYONE SANE BE BITTER? HER WINKS and promises became stock options.

When MercMerge IPOed in November 1999 Trish had six hundred million on paper. She told me to exercise my options—Lloyd wanted it that way. I exercised the options. My three point eight million after taxes looked pretty damn good.

A month later Lloyd's investment firm bought out Herald-Acre International Investments. I heard Lloyd was now worth about five hundred million, on paper. Two days after the buyout I was fired. The golden parachute brought me another five hundred grand. Put everything together, include my 401K and the little stock deal in the Swiss company Samir had forced me to buy, and I had five million bucks, clean, taxed, legitimate.

There were no dreams, no nightmares that left a

residue of peroxide and blood on the tongue, nothing dramatic. No dreams, no nightmares, just money. Only a malcontent would be dissatisfied.

I did something very unlike myself, at least to the Wall Street mind something unlike myself. In January I bought this three-year-old red Ferrari coupe for two hundred thousand cash. I headed west from New York. By the time I got to Utah I had nine speeding tickets, about one per state, each ticket in the three hundred dollar range. In Nevada, U.S. 50 just east of Ely, about four A.M.: I took a long highway curve at one sixty-five, except I didn't quite take it. The gravel spill in my lane was a sudden flash of white and rocks flew like hail and gunfire. The leather-wrapped steering wheel tore from my grip, the car left the road, flipped four times, spun into the desert.

I lay there in the wreck for an hour or so before I tried to move. Then I started trembling. I managed to get through that. I thought I'd broken my back, but everything wriggled right so I knew I'd simply wrenched it. Once I knew I hadn't broken my back I moved because I had to piss and I didn't want to piss in my pants. That's when I discovered my left arm was broken. Yeah, the shock effect was wearing off. Pain replaced the endorphins. Finally, I unhooked my shoulder harness and squirmed from the wreck, a man crawling out of a twisted Italian car.

The winter dawn was cold, gray, the rising sun a rush of bright red and white light that turned the moonscape desert brown. The sun became a quiet fire. Like morning in Saudi, I thought, except colder, with different rocks.

My arm and shoulder started to hurt like unholy hell.

A Nevada state cop saw me standing at the edge of the highway. As he slowed down to talk to me I saw his face through the windshield, his gaze moving from me to the wreck off the highway near the ridge.

His passenger window rolled down. He tipped the brim of his hat back, looked at me, puzzled. "You alone?" the cop asked.

"Yes."

"Vette?"

"Ferrari."

His lips puckered like he wanted to whistle. He didn't whistle. He asked, "How fast were you goin'?"

"One sixty-five."

"That's too fast."

"Yes."

"Where're you goin'?"

I thought for a couple of seconds, then said, "To the hospital?"

The cop grinned. He had a desert sense of humor.

CHAPTER 7

Ted's Funeral

SANTA FE, NEW MEXICO, NEAR THE FRONT WINDOW of a coffee bar the day after the cast came off my arm: I was ignoring the all-news television in the corner, though it lay back there, a low-grade noise. I scratched five-weeks' growth of beard, sipped a latte brewed from beans raised in a Stone Age valley of Irian Jaya. Through the window I watched two Navaho men carry a Persian floor rug out of an antique store and stick it in the back of a white Range Rover.

My head snapped up when the TV's talking head mentioned that an American military officer had been found murdered in Germany. I listened, waited for the anchor to repeat the name. She repeated it. Colonel Theodore Nicholson had been shot and killed in a Berlin alley, near a nightclub in the old eastern zone.

Now the TV had my total attention. A file tape of the Brandenburg Gate flashed across the screen followed by a long pan down the Ku'damm. Then the network cut live to a reporter on a drab, narrow street of gray and brown buildings. Stodgy German police stood in the background, the evening shadows broken by spinning red and blue emergency lights. As the reporter spoke, a picture of the deceased appeared on-screen—a man in uniform, a grinning man with a big nose. The picture removed all doubt. The reporter said Colonel Nicholson's body would be flown back to the U.S. for burial in Arlington National Cemetery. The network returned to its Washington studios. The next ten minutes of airtime included two Washington experts speculating about Ted's murder. They mentioned Kurd terrorism, German neo-Nazi terrorism, Islamic fundamentalist terrorism, a Serbian nationalist hit team, international drug cartels, the usual suspects.

My latte had turned to cold suds.

I left the bar, walked down the street to my hotel, packed my bag, checked out. I drove my rental Toyota to the Albuquerque airport, turned it in, had the agency reserve a compact in D.C. I bought a one-way ticket to Washington, Reagan National.

FORTY-EIGHT HOURS LATER THE UNITED STATES OF America buried Ted, at high noon on a bright, windy, chilly March day.

I barely knew Renee, his wife. Ted and I had been close, as professional soldiers doing a job are close. I'd met Renee only once, right after she and Ted married in 1987. I was in Stuttgart for a conference at European Command. At the officers' club Ted introduced me to his blonde Belgian wife.

At the funeral Renee wore sunglasses, a dark blue dress, her twin seven-year-old sons standing beside her.

Civilians from State, the Department of Defense, civilians from who knows what government agency mixed with a lot of uniforms and a hefty dose of media. I counted eleven video cams, saw at least two dozen identifiable reporters. I noticed a cute redhead wearing black, a reporter I'd seen on cable. A number of big-time Foreign Service officers and midlevel dignitaries from European, Arab, African, and South Asian embassies mixed in the crowd. Most of the FSOs and the embassy reps wore name tags.

I drifted, listening to the chatter. There wasn't much whodunnit buzz. Those discussions had already occurred back at the embassy or in the office, but friends bump into friends and in English-dominated America even highly experienced diplomats occasionally think their native language is a safe, undecipherable code, a cocoon for communication American dumbshits won't comprehend.

I overheard enough of two conversations, before I participated in a third. The first encounter was short and utterly coincidental, but it shook me. It was a scream of "Hey, dumb ass, wake the hell up."

I was in the rear of the assembling crowd, near the sidewalk. A French lieutenant colonel, in dress uniform, passed me, speaking quickly into his mobile phone. You know how large crowds work, people aren't random atoms. Cells of people migrate. A minute later I was behind the French officer, and near the shoulder of a woman in a gray overcoat. She was five five, her brown hair back in a stiff bun. The French officer shot a quick glance at me, my scrag beard, longish hair, cheap sunglasses, brown leather jacket and blue tie. He leaned toward the woman and whispered in French, "So, Dominique, will you tell me why he was murdered now?"

"Shut the fuck up, Ro-bert," she replied in a tart Parisian accent.

Then she flicked a cutter glance at me. I was just ahead of her, stooping to tie my unlaced right shoe like I didn't have a clue. From the corner of my eye I caught her—the hard brown eyes, sharp nose, the athletic angles of her tanned face—the woman Elise Neaves had met on the pier in Aruba.

My fingers failed to complete the loop of my shoelace.

Dominique. This close she was much more attractive.

Her eyes moved from me to Robert.

I swallowed hard. I tried to tie the lace again. I was impressed. French intelligence always manages to find and field attractive female athletes with genius IQs and the morals of a Hells Angels biker bitch.

Dominique jerked her head to the left. Robert understood the signal. The Dominique and Robert tête-à-tête moved.

I finished with the shoelace, then stood. Fascinating, I thought. I had several instant theories.

A man bumped me in the shoulder, said excuse me. I stepped aside as two Arab gentlemen took the space Dominique and Robert had vacated. I saw their name tags, one from Jordan and the other from Kuwait. The Jordanian and the Kuwaiti were clearly two friends who had just run into one another. Their what's-going-on in Oxford English quickly turned to Arabic gossip about the funeral. The puffy-faced Jordanian said he'd heard

Nicholson had a spot of bad luck. Nicholson went to the Berlin nightclub to meet a Czech girlfriend when—so unfortunate—a drug hit aimed at a Turk dealer occurred. What've you heard, Amal? the Jordanian asked. A Czech girlfriend, huh? the Kuwaiti mused. That's a twist, little sex to it after all, eh? And drugs? Possibly rock and roll, too, at the club? Actually, the Kuwaiti continued, I hear guns and rhinestones. Rhinestones? the Jordanian asked. Yes, the Kuwaiti said. The police found rhinestones stuffed in his mouth. Nicholson went to the nightclub to talk to a Turk dealer involved in a gunrunning operation, an operation somewhere in the Balkans. Or perhaps Cyprus. The Kuwaiti paused, eyed his friend. Rhinestones? the Jordanian asked again. Rhinestones in his mouth? Why rhinestones in his mouth? The Kuwaiti responded with a dunno shrug.

The Arabs quit talking. The color guard marched into the field. I turned around, checking on *ma chèrie* Dominique and her darling Robert. That's when I saw standing behind me two East African men. The shorter man, thin and slightly graying at the temples, looked at me. I looked at him and recognized him.

No eavesdropping here—I spoke to him. "I'm Pete Ford," I said. "Isn't your name Mosoke? Louis Mosoke?"

"Yes." Though his look was careful and cautious, he extended his hand politely. I shook it.

"I believe we met in Nairobi. . . . You're Ugandan, aren't you?"

"Yes."

"You're here with the embassy?"

"Yes . . . I'm very sorry. I—I don't remember you."

"I was temporarily attached to the American embassy in Kenya, eighty-seven. I was in the military, didn't have a beard."

He grinned. "Oh . . . oh yes."

"You knew Ted Nicholson?"

"Yes." Mosoke nodded. He looked away from me, momentarily, toward the honor guard. "When he was in Kampala," Mosoke added.

I started to say I'd done a little of Kampala, when Ambassador Everett Kilean was there, but I didn't. You never know how someone's going to react if you mention Everett.

"What do you do now, Mr. Ford?" Mosoke asked.

"I was with an investment firm in New York. Herald-Acre—it was bought out a couple of months ago." I grinned, touched my beard. "I'm looking for a job, at my own pace."

"You got a nice settlement?"

I shrugged. "The MercMerge IPO was better."

Mosoke smiled. "MercMerge, that was a deal. Haf you a card?" he asked with sudden interest.

"No. At the moment I'm without E-mail, and I don't have a telephone."

"*Soooo*—you are ree-jeck-ting both the twentieth and twenty-first centuries?"

"I've no telegraph, so I'm repudiating the nineteenth as well."

Mosoke's eyes sparkled. He wasn't finished with the repartee. "We use *drums,* Mr. Ford, in parts of Africa."

"Mr. Mosoke, I don't even own a bongo."

Mosoke chuckled. The other African, the tall, raw-boned man standing on the far side of Mosoke, the guy who had to be a Dinka, a tall man so calm, so easy in his blue suit and tie, grinned.

For a moment the Dinka and I stared at one another. His amused grin faded, not a fade with malice. His lips, his cheeks stiffened with a grim pride. He knew what caught my attention: the scar tissue up the back of his neck and beneath his left ear, whitened, gnarled, the leftover of an encounter with high explosives. I wanted to ask him, "When were you wounded, sir? Was it artillery shrapnel or a land mine?"—but I knew, at the moment, the question was completely inappropriate.

Mosoke hasn't introduced us, I thought. Well, play it as if it were an oversight.

"Pete Ford," I said, extending him my hand.

"Pil-dee," he replied. His grip crunched my hand bones. The guy had huge fingers.

"You knew Colonel Nicholson?"

"Yes . . . quite well." Then he added, "He was a good friend."

"Are you Dinka?" I asked.

Pildi glanced at Mosoke then looked back at me. The sly grin returned. "I am."

"From south Sudan?"

"So you know East Africa, Mr. Ford. . . . At one time, yes, near Nimule. Do you know of it?"

"Yes. Refugee camp. Sudan Peoples Liberation Army base area."

"You do know Nimule. . . . Now I am a major in the Ugandan Army, Mr. Ford."

I glanced at Mosoke. He was stone-faced, absorbing everything I said, observing everything I did. I looked back at Pildi. "Don't answer this, Major Pildi, if you think it's too forward, I know you don't know me, we met here at this funeral, but I know Ted did some advising with your army's senior intelligence section." I let the sentence hang, implying the question. He could answer it if he wanted to, or plead ignorance.

His eyes narrowed, the malarial yellow in them showing, but he answered it. "You are well-informed, Mr. Ford," Major Pildi said, softly but so distinctly.

We made excellent eye contact.

Pildi said, "Nicholson helped me with a *vexing* aircraft problem."

I had to think about that. It could mean several things. I was surprised Pildi would say something so potentially suggestive and indiscreet.

Pildi read my mind. "Perhaps from your point of view that's classified," he said, giving Mosoke a glance. Mosoke nodded, an okay. "As you might guess, I have complicated interests. But that is Africa, isn't it? Your friend Nicholson could understand and act, to aid us amid those complexities. . . . He's dead now, and *I* can thank him for the risks he took on behalf of the *abandoned* and the *ignored.*"

The dose of bitterness made me wait a second, but I had to ask, had to nail it so I knew and didn't have to assume. "The vexing aircraft, Pildi. Were they Khartoum government planes bombing Dinka villages?"

"Again, you are *well* informed, Mr. Ford."

"That was a guess. I'm not an intelligence officer."

"Then you made an astute guess."

"Are you at the embassy here in Washington, Major?"

He glanced at Mosoke again before he said, "I'm temporarily in New York, at the United Nations. The peacekeeping force discussions for Congo, I am peripherally involved with those particulars."

I nodded. "That's a complicated mess."

Pildi nodded, started to reply, but there was a brief, noxious *brat* of microphone feedback. Pildi looked up, over my head, as he said, "We should discuss it, Mr. Ford. In my opinion the Congo War is a criminal undertaking stoked by greedy bastards in Africa and Europe."

That's when Mosoke nudged me. "Here," Mosoke said. The diplomatic stone face was gone, replaced by diplomatic hustle. He put one of his cards in my hand, said with a soft smile, "Please, in case you wish to communicate? I am always interested in speaking with investment bankers who have had *real* experience in East Africa." Now he nodded toward the front. "We should face around, Mr. Ford. The ceremony is beginning."

THEY BURIED TED. THE HONOR GUARD FIRED THE final salute. The wind had been sneaking around all morning, and, as if the blank rifle shots were its cue, it whipped up cold and brisk. As the color sergeant gave Renee the Stars and Stripes off the casket, the breeze tore at her dress.

Mosoke and Pildi shook hands with me again, then left. One of them had a plane to catch. They didn't say which one, but I guessed it was Pildi.

The wind played hell throughout the brief reception. They'd strung a white tent over a section of sidewalk, and it flapped and popped. You couldn't whisper with that wind blowing, and shouted condolences don't convey the best tones of sympathy. I got in line, when my turn came I introduced myself to Renee, tried to whisper an I'm-sorry in her ear. She thanked me, said she guessed she'd be looking for a job in Virginia, said she planned to take the boys to see her parents in Belgium, in Antwerp, but as her fingers tightened on my wrist, her tough-gal face collapsed and she burst into tears. I barely knew her, but now I knew her, so I hugged her. She had that empty tremble, hollow bones. "Ted always talked about you, Pete, how sad he was you left the service," she said. She looked at me, through streaming blue eyes. Somebody gave her a handkerchief. "These are my boys, Pete," she said. I met her twins. The boys were still in shock, so pale these baby-faced replicas of Ted.

As I left the tent the breeze whipped all the flags, the huge flags on the tall steel poles, the little flags on wooden stakes marking the graves. I said a prayer for Renee and her boys. I crossed myself. I hadn't done that in a while.

I DIDN'T WASTE TIME LOOKING FOR DOMINIQUE AND Lieutenant Colonel Robert. I've told you what I heard, Dominique, the Arabs, Pildi and Mosoke. I won't say I knew anything. I had sketchy facts, increasing curiosity, and an anger I didn't understand but knew wouldn't disappear.

From the reception I headed for my rental car. I'd parked south, which, if you know Arlington, means a long walk to the lots. You walk past the graves, the beautifully kept graves, and you think and you feel. You can't help but think about a line like *"Will you tell me why he was murdered now, Dominique?"* You don't sit on your ass when you hear that. Even if it's not your job, you think, you develop possibilities, analyze courses of action, see the awful implications. Arlington's beautiful graves, the green lawn of American dead—even if you can supply superb objective analysis about cause and effect and history and motive you can't help but feel and begin to feel too much. Renee's comment chewed on me. *"Ted always talked about you, Pete, how sad he was you left the service."* She had to say that to me? Of course I knew why she said it. Renee simply repeated what she'd heard. She's just lost her husband to a killer, I'm a name from his past and son of a bitch, that's what Ted had said about Pete Ford. QED. Except I doubt he used the "sad." Ted would have griped, described himself as pissed off, disgusted, and disappointed with that self-absorbed Peter Ford.

Rhinestones in his mouth. Superb African contacts. Too much . . .

As I reached the rental car I considered the rhinestones. If it was true Ted had rhinestones crammed in his mouth then that indicated an assassination with a message. No big guess to figure rhinestones as a substitute for diamonds. I made that leap the second I heard the Kuwaiti mention the rhinestones, but I had to think about it, play with it, keep thinking about it when I was talking to a Ugandan intelligence officer that had to know a great deal about diamond smuggling. Though there was another angle. Rhinestones are also fake, they're paste. Maybe they weren't a diamond substitute. But if they weren't meant to represent diamonds, what's the deal? Though it was none of my business I had to know if the rhinestone bit was true. The Germans, CIA, FBI would investigate this. Thanks to Dominique, extraordinary coincidence, and Robert's loose lips, I had indications French intel was interested.

I slid into the driver's seat of the Chevy. I won't say

I knew. I can't say I knew. The angry part of me wanted this to tie into Jumpsuit and the atrocities. That want was my own sense of disgrace and desire for a crack at redemption. What a selfish thing to make out of Ted's murder. I was embarrassed. I put the key in the ignition.

Dominique, the fire on the *Peace Warrior* and Ted's funeral. My old man didn't believe in either luck or coincidence. According to him there's no such thing as luck, if you're a pro who puts in the time and effort. My father once told me that the most useful embassy employees understood their job included hanging out, working crowds, observing and listening. Facts feed intelligence analysts but nuance feeds politics, my father said, and politics deals with future actions and objectives. The electronic and image intel people get lots of details, those kinds of facts, but the nuance, the facial expressions, the subtle gesture, the insight from encounters that are the intended result of being on the ground and in the crowd—these are the dynamic means of making sense of the details, of detecting impending action. Nuance requires a human presence in a country or among a people, a trained, professional, and patient human observer. Working crowds, hanging out, at times these can be dangerous activities, Pete, but usually they're simply boring. But you never know when the effort will prove to be fruitful. That's why, wherever you are, look, listen. Certain kinds of events will attract familiar faces. Remember them. When you see them again it won't be luck or coincidence.

He may have been a useless son of a bitch but Dad knew his business.

I started the Chevy, pumped the gas.
Rhinestones in his mouth.
Had Ted been tortured?
I put the car in gear and pulled away from the curb.

CHAPTER 8

I WENT TO AN INTERNET CAFÉ IN ALEXANDRIA AND sat down at a computer. I wanted everything the Net and wire services had on Ted's murder. The computer spat out twenty-six stories on Ted's murder, several from European papers, no mention of rhinestones. The latest facts: Ted's body had been found in the street in front of the nightclub, two bullets in his head. No one saw the assailant. The cops thought the body had been dumped but no one saw a car. Ted wasn't in uniform when he was killed, which could mean something or nothing. The U.S. embassy refused comment on a rumor that Ted was meeting (or arranging a meeting) with a Kurdish dissident, a former Kurd guerrilla wanted on murder charges in Turkey. One German report in particular had an authentic, between-the-lines feel. An unidentified source in the Turkish embassy in Germany had told Munich's *Suddeutsche Zeitung* that he believed the Kurd terrorist (terrorist, not dissident, was the official Turk characterization) whom Nicholson intended to meet had indicated he planned to accept Ankara's generous offer of qualified amnesty and would surrender to Turk authorities. Why the terrorist would speak with an American military officer prior to surrender was not clear. The Turks declined to provide a name for the Kurd leader but the story said another anonymous source identified the man as Turan Bozlak. I noted the name of the German reporter, Ursala Heiden.

Kurds inhabit southeastern Turkey, parts of western Iran, a slice of Syria and lots of northern Iraq. Northern Iraq was European Command's beat. I disagreed with the Turk spokesman. Ted could have had several good reasons to meet Bozlak. It might be simple. Bozlak could have been a regular informant.

On an Internet "find everybody and anybody" search engine I plugged in R. B. Guyton's name. I wanted a set of the Jumpsuit photos, for myself. Guyton generated ninety-seven hits. No, not ninety-seven R. B. Guytons, ninety-seven hits mentioning *the* R. B. Guyton. A dozen web pages reviewed a book of his war photos that had been published in Europe, titled *Neutral Density*. Amazon, Barnes & Noble, and strategypage.com, all of them gave Guyton's war photo work a thumbs-up. I went to Guyton's web page, which listed an agent in New York. I jotted down the phone number.

I drove back over the river into the District. I didn't go to my hotel. I went to the Smithsonian and looked at airplanes and spacecraft for a couple of hours. At least I tried to look at airplanes and spacecraft. What I did was walk around the X-15, stare at the *Spirit of St. Louis,* stand near a P-38, and think about Ted's murder.

I GOT BACK TO MY HOTEL AROUND SEVEN, HAD A
steak in the restaurant. About eight I phoned Ambassador Kilean's office at State. Ev's got a full-time secretary, one who screens his calls even when he's at his
home in Annandale.

She put me through to his home. When he answered
I said, "I want something from you."

Kilean replied, easily, "Come over to the house and
join me for a drink. Single malt. It isn't poison."

I crossed on the Chain, took the Parkway to the
Loop, got off on Little River Turnpike. Kilean had five
acres on Woodlark, surrounded by a black, wrought-
iron fence studded with sensors and trip lights.

He met me at the door, his poker face positioned, a
crystal glass with ice and scotch in his left hand, his
right hand in his chino pants pocket. As he took a sip of
whiskey and rattled the ice, his gray eyebrows creased,
a break in the poker face. He was wondering if I'd be a
prick and not shake his hand. I stuck my hand out.
"Good," he said as we shook. Good, like he was relieved. He said "Let's go into my office."

Polished cherry wood paneled the home office. A
large window, stroked with iron bars, exposed a dark,
inner courtyard. One small light lit the courtyard,
enough to reveal the silhouettes of marble statues and
the presence of an ivy-trailing oak.

A brief scowl marred Kilean's gray, thin, autocrat's
face. "Scotch, Pete?" he asked. "It's smooth." He nodded at the scotch bottle on his wide mahogany desk.

"I'll pass."

"I can get you orange juice? No? . . . Care to sit
down?"

I sat.

"I've heard from friends in on the MercMerge IPO. They tell me I did them a huge favor. What was it, an instant four billion in market value? I didn't invest, dammit. . . . You must have done quite well."

"I didn't," I replied. "I thought I made it clear I was helping out a friend."

"You did. . . . Your beard . . . it isn't Herald-Acre."

"I was fired, Ev."

Ambassador Kilean thought a moment, took a sip of whiskey. He knew damn well I wasn't going to ask him for a job.

I said, "Let's talk about Ted Nicholson's murder."

He blinked. He said, "A current topic." I think he started to add "son" but he didn't.

Everett stood beside his huge mahogany desk and peered through the barred window. His head craned forward, slightly, his gray hair slick in the office's hushed light. "I've acquired a new sculpture, a magnificent kouros," he said, nodding toward the courtyard. "Second century A.D. Roman reproduction of sixth century B.C. Greek. I've placed it in the hallway off the courtyard. May I show it to you?" He flipped a light switch beside the bookshelf, turned toward me, his upper teeth on his lower lip.

I could see the statue, tall, lucent marble in the new, bright cone of light. "Did you get it through a Lebanese or Turk source?" I asked.

"Lebanese."

"One of Dad's artifact smugglers?"

Everett replied with a nod. He didn't smile.

"Let's discuss Colonel Nicholson, Ev."

The ambassador sat down at his desk, in his padded leather chair, reached over and picked up the scotch bottle. As he poured a fresh slug into his glass he said, "Okay, Colonel Ted Nicholson . . . I'm not going to ask you why you want to know. I've no doubts you're well motivated." He allowed the briefest hint of irony.

I didn't like the hint. "I understand orphans," I replied.

Kilean frowned, considered going there, then didn't. Then he did. "Touché," he said, with frost.

Our eyes locked.

He broke the gaze, looked at the wall. To drink or not to drink, the thought ripped his brain, telegraphed by the lip tremor any child of an alcoholic immediately decodes. The answer's always the same. Kilean took a slurp. He put the glass down, the scotch respite buying the old cad ten seconds to compose himself. "Sometime, Pete, I would like to try—" he looked back at me "—and discuss *all* of it. . . . Could we do that, with no gimmicks?"

"We could . . . but not tonight. Let's talk Nicholson."

Everett looked—well, he looked relieved, again. "All right," he said, "not tonight . . . but we're going to do it."

"Yes."

He tapped the desktop with his finger. "Since Nicholson's murder is hot we'll have to play wink and nod. You tell me what you have, first."

I went with the story from the German newspaper I'd pulled from the Internet.

He nodded, stiffly. "The German press reports have got what we've got, since they got it from us. He definitely wasn't shot there, though. His body was dumped. He'd been dead about an hour when they found him."

"Who found him?"

"Manager of the club at the end of that street. Only business there. It's one of those old East Berlin districts that's about to be renovated. Fine place to drop a body if you don't want to be seen dropping it."

"What about the killer's weapons?"

"Nine millimeter pistol fired from close range, left powder burns. We think the rounds were self-loaded, some suggestive crimping on the recovered slugs. Penetration suggests they were subsonic."

"Your facts suggest a pro."

"Not necessarily, not with all of the weaponry available. Punks can get anything the KGB had. Buy it off the Internet from unemployed assassins."

"How come Ted's wife and kids weren't with him in Berlin?"

"No scheme there, I think," he replied. "The simple answer is Germany was a new assignment. Nicholson'd spent a special yearlong tour at the embassy in Uganda, so his wife, being sane, kept her kids here in Virginia. She's Belgian, you know. In fact, right before he was murdered, Nicholson saw his father-in-law, in Antwerp. We've already contacted him, talked with him—her father, I mean. Nicholson discussed family business with his father-in-law, moving his wife and sons. Interesting people, though, her family, the Michauds? Diamond merchants, cutters."

"Diamonds?"

"Yes."

"What was Ted doing in Uganda?"

"Pinch-hitting." Kilean grasped the scotch bottle, poured as he said, "State Department had him moving. Nicholson was observing in Angola for a while, the cease-fire that wasn't. That *mess* in the Congo—you want a job? I could use you right now. Monitor a non-existent cease-fire."

That's how Kilean worked in a job pitch, smooth like it was a fresh discovery. I ignored the pitch. I asked, "What's your best guess as to motive?"

"Motive?"

"Why kill Ted, Ambassador? Was he handling something dangerous?"

Everett's eyebrows crunched into a taut, broad vee. "Not in the way of official business. All of us in the trade make enemies, I don't need to tell you that. Nicholson—look, he seemed to be running an unofficial investigation. Wildcat's never a wise idea." Everett raised his glass, inspected the scotch, the rich brown smoke of the single malt. "Damn. I may as well tell you. That's not speculation, really. The day he was killed he told our station chief he thought he might have something relating to war crimes, something important. That's what he said, that it was important. There are only four people who know that. You're number four."

"Five won't hear it from me."

"I know."

"The war crimes . . . what war crimes?"

"The most obvious figure is that Kurd, Bozlak. If he was meeting Bozlak, you'd think crimes in Turkey or the Balkans, Bosnia or Kosovo perhaps. Even Iraq."

"Iraq?" I asked.

I think my harsh tone surprised Everett. "Kurdistan, northern Iraq? Saddam gassed the Kurds. . . . I'm guessing, Pete. Nicholson filed a number of war crimes reports in Africa, official reports from Angola. He went into the Democratic Republic of Congo occasionally, with Ugandan Army officers. Those trips were . . . his reports from Congo are unofficial."

"You remember a war crime I reported, at the end of Desert Storm?"

"Yes . . . The nurse . . . Whatever happened with that?"

"You might look into it."

Kilean reflected a moment. "You think—" he started. Then he said, as he thought it through. "Okay, I'll do that."

"I want to read Ted's war crime reports, the ones you mentioned."

"He was murdered. Everything's close hold."

"I want to read them."

Everett tapped the desk with his finger. "I haven't read them. . . . Obviously, you think I should."

"Turks and Germans know where Bozlak's at?"

"If they do they haven't told us." He scowled, then he quelled the scowl with another sip of whiskey.

"What about the French, Everett?"

He gave me a quizzical look. "Why do you think they'd be involved? The Congo business?"

I told him no. I told him what I'd overheard at the funeral, the exchange between Dominique and Robert. Everett leaned over the desk, intensely interested. "Dominique Cadeau? *She's* here in Washington? Give it to me, again." I described the woman a second time, fully and completely. "Damn. That's her. Or her sister." Everett's gray-blue eyes became bright devils. He rapped the desktop with delight and blurted out in spook jargon, "Cadeau's a trigger puller, Pete, for The Swimming Pool. Do you remember the scuttling of that peacenik boat in Aruba, the antinuclear protests? She burned the *EcoClash!* sloop. Really screwed her mission. Word was she got rattled over something, was supposed to damage the boat, not *burn* the damn thing. Her masters stuck her down in French Guiana for a while to chill. Told *EcoClash!* she'd been imprisoned. Shows you, doesn't it, Peter, *everybody* has a crappy night." My eyes bugged, but he missed it. He chuckled, shook his head again, finally took a sip of his scotch, his eyes narrowing slightly as he said, "Now, clue me, what— what's *she* doing at Ted Nicholson's funeral?"

I reminded Kilean that knowing the answer to that was his job, or FBI counterintel's job.

I also cracked a smile. Everett's spy jargon dated him. One of the main French DGSE offices overlooks the public swimming pool in the Parc des Tourelles. DGSE: Direction Générale de la Sécurité Extérieure, France's CIA. Hence, to old guard CIA like Kilean and my father, the DSGE and its predecessor, the SDECE, were called The Swimming Pool—*la piscine.*

"I'll inquire, first thing tomorrow. Dominique Cadeau. You show up and bump in to her. Kid," Everett chuckled, "you inherited the knack." From the glint in his eye I think he wanted to make a comment about Dad. Instead, he added, "I owe you another one. You've another chit."

I decided, since he was so relaxed, to gamble. No, not about Dominique's screwup in Aruba, that I understood, but the rhinestones. "Let me cash the chit, Ambassador. I overheard two Arab diplomats talking at the funeral. One told the other that Ted's mouth was filled with rhinestones. You haven't mentioned that, it's not in any of the papers."

Kilean shook his head, an I-don't-believe-it shake.

But that didn't last long since he could believe it. He said, quietly, "There was a diamond in his mouth and one in his stomach."

"Cut or uncut?"

"Uncut."

"Have you run an analysis on the stones?"

"Son, what the hell *don't* you know?"

"Answer my question."

"They're . . . we're doing it now."

"You might be able to identify the source, the mine, there's a laser test technique."

"Peter — are you here to pull my leg? Are you working for somebody?"

"Of course not."

"*Would* I know if you were?"

"Yes. . . . Did you lase the diamonds?"

"We did, but my experts tell me at the moment the database is small, especially for riverine diamonds. . . . We could get lucky."

"Do you think, like I do, they're embargoed diamonds, Ev? Blood diamonds? From where? Where are they from? Angola, Congo?"

Kilean nodded, a curt yes.

"How big was the stone Ted swallowed?"

"Six carats, and likely of very high quality . . . The coroner found a two-carat under his tongue so they looked for others. I'm told the big one showed up on X ray or MRI. Looked like a golf ball."

"You might be able to talk with a two-carat stone in your mouth but a six-carat is a speech impediment."

"Pete, there's no indication he was bound, physically, no marks on his wrists, no sign of torture."

"No drugs?"

"No."

"His father-in-law is a diamond cutter?"

"We've followed up on that."

"*You* said you talked to him about *family* matters."

Kilean flashed barracuda teeth. He cooled for ten seconds before he replied: "Fuck you, Peter. I tell you, you *ever* work for anybody, you work for me."

I didn't reply.

"Okay, kid, here you go. . . . Monsieur Michaud says Nicholson showed him five uncut diamonds and asked him if he could identify their origin. Nicholson told his father-in-law he thought they were Angolan. He wasn't sure. Michaud says he examined the diamonds and said he could not be sure, but he had cut Angolan stones and they could be Angolan stones." Kilean took a sip of scotch, then added, "As you know, most Angolan diamonds, except those from the government's Cuago mine, are blood diamonds. They're embargoed by the United Nations, to try and stop the rebels from selling the stones to buy weapons."

The ugly thought had already crossed my mind and I didn't flinch from it. "Ted Nicholson was one of the best. But I gotta ask. Any indication Ted was smuggling?"

"No. None."

"But you're checking?"

"That's the job, kiddo."

"He didn't ask his father-in-law to fence a few stones?"

"Oh come on. Would Michaud tell anyone that?"

"But Michaud said he was shown five diamonds and there were two on Ted."

"That's what he said."

"Anyone watching Michaud?"

"We've asked for help from the Belgians. The old man is retired and as Belgian diamond men go, he has an honest reputation."

"Three diamonds missing . . . this could be a simple robbery and murder."

"You don't seem to think so, Peter."

"Do you think this is about Kurds and Turks, Ambassador?"

"We can't rule anything out, Peter."

"No . . . no, sir, you're quite right. *You* can't."

CHAPTER 9

R. B. Guyton

I HAD BREAKFAST AT NINE THE NEXT MORNING, THEN
I called my accountant in New York. Marlene blistered
my ear. That pushy Samir had called her four times in
the last two days, trying to find me. She ripped me for
not telling her I'd left Santa Fe. She said my mail had
piled up at my apartment. Yeah, she was paying my
bills, I'd better pay her bill. She told me to get my butt
up to New York so I could sign my tax returns.

I phoned Samir. He was still at Herald-Acre — Lloyd
wasn't fool enough to fire him. During the conversation
Samir and I talked about several things, office things, a
new client, but the presumably big items — the way it
looked then — were R. B. Guyton and Samir's news
about his estranged brother, Alain.

"This fren' of yours, Mr. Guy-tone. He has called
from Paris five times in the last few days."

"Sam — Guyton called you, for me?"

"Fran slips me your calls now, Peter. Many of our clients, they still want to reach you, and they complained, yes?"

"I could've been reached. Except for maybe a couple of weeks in Nevada."

"For a little time your calls went to Mr. Lloyd, eh? So, no more, Fran and I have rearranged that. I tell our clients you are my consultant. It works best that way. We've a potential new client who wants to meet with you. I spoke to him yesterday. You do not object, do you? May I regard you as my consultant?"

"Okay, I'm a consultant. What'd Guyton want?"

"Mr. Guy-tone said he tried to reach you at your apartment and he knew you worked here. He seemed . . . he was highly *tense,* Peter. I told him you were on extended holiday."

"You get an address and phone?"

Samir gave me Guyton's address and phone. "And Peter," he added, a new delight in his voice. "My brother, Alain. We're seeing one another."

"The priest?"

"No. Alain's the businessman, in Istanbul. I received a fax from him, in Rome. He's there for a conference. He asked me if I would come join him. He must have an old letterhead, because he asked if you were still my boss. . . . Have you ever come across my brother?"

"No, not that I recall."

"Well, I spoke with a secretary in Rome. I called immediately, told him to tell Alain I would come. I'm going to leave tomorrow. This is good news, Peter. My prodigal brother meets many interesting people. Entrée, you know. Perhaps new clients and information."

I told Samir it was great to talk to someone who had

good news. As for the rest of the conversation—I heard about all of our clients. I even heard about Fran the receptionist's latest face-lift.

I CALLED GUYTON. THE PHONE RANG SIX TIMES THEN an answering machine came on, a sultry woman's voice speaking French. No names, just leave a message. I left a message, my name, no number, said I'd call back later in the day.

I checked out of the hotel, caught a shuttle flight to New York. I went by my apartment in the East Village, dumped my bags. About two in the afternoon I saw Marlene, signed the tax returns, looked at all my statements. "You're not doing bad," Marlene said. She was right. My portfolio was back over five million.

I tried Guyton again, from her office phone.

This time he answered.

"RB? Pete Ford?"

There was a surprising breathlessness. "Hey—I been tryin' to get aholt of you, whole week."

"That's what I heard."

Did I know what was coming? No—but damn, it felt like I was living out my own theory, like history was written and I knew next week's lottery number.

Guyton said, "Yeah. Hey, Colonel Nicholson, the man kilt in Berlin? You hear about that shit? You remember I met him in Saudi, you sent me to Corps?"

Even if I knew the lottery number, my gut tightened like I was sick with surprise. "Of course I remember. I remember your phone call in 1994, when you flew through Boston."

Guyton paused, like he suddenly remembered. He

said, "Hey, uh, guess I shoulda ast you how you're doing, huh? We ain't talked in years."

"RB, I went to Nicholson's funeral this afternoon. If this is about Nicholson, let's talk about Nicholson."

"Shit . . . yeah . . . yeah, that's it." He sounded worried.

"So talk about Nicholson."

"I uh . . . Maybe we shouldn't talk, on the phone, you know? You get me? Maybe I'll send you stuff overnight, huh?"

He's worried about phone security, I thought. Still, I was too interested. I asked, "What kind of stuff?"

"Look . . . I run into him when I'm in Bosnia, you know, working for *Newsweek,* so Nicholson knows how to get aholt of me? He called a year ago, wanted more copies of some photos. He calls the man Jumpsuit. . . . Hey, you there?"

"Of course I'm here."

"Ted and me—he was, when we were talking, arguing. Like, last week, he said, where you come in again, he said what you'd cooked up—"

I'd heard enough. Damn, I thought, *last week.* "Listen RB, we can't—"

"Doan interrupt me, I'll get there, man. Shit, there's *so* much. Two months ago, I'm in Prague. I'm settin'—"

"Guyton," I shouted. *"Stop."*

He shut up, midsentence and cold. You could hear a moment of satellite static, orbiting clicks.

I said, "You're right. . . . This is not a phone conversation."

There was another pause, more satellite static. He said, softly, "That's what I was *tryin'* to say."

We were both silent for long enough to feel it.

I said, "I'll fly over there, tomorrow. I can do it. . . . I need to do it."

"Good . . . Pete, there's too much, see? . . . I could be in the States, but, uh, I have props?"

"Props?"

"Gimme a better nonword," he replied. Then he added, "We shouldna sat on our ass."

"No. They were lousy orders."

"I seen some others, in the Balkans," RB muttered. "There's a condition photographers need. Detachment . . . But between you and me, like at the river, there are those times a camera just doesn't fuckin' cut it."

THE NEXT MORNING I BOUGHT A TICKET TO PARIS, A late flight that night, to arrive in France in the early afternoon. I also made a reservation on a flight from Paris to Berlin. I called Marlene then called Samir, said I was going to Paris, that they could reach me at Guyton's.

That afternoon, before I went to JFK, I called Kilean's office, the one he uses at State. His secretary put me through to him.

"I'm traveling," I said.

"I thought you might."

"The war crime I witnessed, Ev. What have you got you can tell me over an unsecure line?"

"Well, I can tell you it isn't a closed case, Peter. . . . I received a copy of your After Action Report, a memo from McCullar, a follow-up memo from Nicholson, all dating from 1991. One photo went out on the wire in 1991. According to this file, no feedback."

I considered telling him about Guyton but decided to wait on it until I knew what Guyton had. Even though the line was unsecure I asked, "Any news on my *swimmer?*"

"Nothing . . . Peter—do we stay in touch, this time?"

Christ. I realized I'd almost forgiven the man. I said "Sure."

"You have my numbers—the E-mail?"

"Yes."

"Should I have to reach you, Pete, how should I do it?"

I thought about it before I said it. "Could you leave a message with Dr. Gunther?"

Kilean asked, with no particular emotion, "You mean, leave a message with the Brussels office of Hospital for Humanity?"

I said yes, that's what I meant.

"All right," he replied, stiffly.

I could tell he hadn't quite forgiven himself.

GUYTON'S PLACE IN PARIS. RUE DE BIEVRE, 5TH ARrondissement. Street construction forced the cabbie to stop and drop me off a couple of blocks away. Pulling my roller bag, I passed a French cop standing next to a postered kiosk. He perused a poster, complete with lyrics, of a rock band from Bosnia whose music ruled Paris.

A moment later I was looking up a corridor of four- and five-story brick and stone town houses, the top of the Pantheon visible above the roofs at the end of the narrow street.

RB lived in a four-story town house, one with a Belle Epoque feel, pale yellow paint on stone, the second, third and fourth floors marked with imposing grated windows. The ubiquitous French key code box—*Le Code*—stood next to the huge carved double door, a door with a massive black iron door knocker. An opaque, anodized orb sat on a ledge over the door arch. I figured it held a closed-circuit TV camera. I punched the buzzer in the code box, didn't hear anything, so I raised the knocker and slammed it.

A voice snapped over the hidden intercom: "Yeah?"

"RB?"

"Naw." The voice asked, "You Ford?"

"Yes." I heard a trundling step beyond the door, followed by a series of smooth, mechanical sounds. The door creaked open.

She was exotic—fairly tall, rawboned, rounded nose, hair cut to inch-length all around her skull. Mousse or wax coiffed the hair into stiff waves and odd spikes. She wore a Chicago Bulls T-shirt, the fierce bull logo punched forward by two full, hard breasts. Jet black mascara, oceanic eyeliner, hot red lipstick, purple denim cowboy jacket with silver buttons, purple boots and purple leather pants completed the ensemble.

The woman leaned against the huge door, and the way she leaned suggested she had well-developed arm and shoulder muscles, buff and hefty. She cracked a wad of chewing gum and said, in English, faint suggestion of a Southern accent, "Nifty weather, huh?" She looked me up and down. "Come on in."

"Is RB here?"

She nodded, cracked her gum again. "I'm Liss-ta. You're Pete, huh?" She put an index finger—a long fingernail, purple nail polish—against my shoulder, moved the finger down my arm. "Studsy . . ." She rolled her tongue against her lips. A louche gaze filled Lissta's eyes as she said, "Upstairs, third floor."

HE WAS WAITING AT THE TOP OF THE STAIRS. EXCEPT for the jazz dot beard on his chin, RB hadn't changed. He was skinny. His haircut met basic training standards. The open leather vest he wore showed bare chest and a six-pack abdomen. No diamond earrings, no tattoos, no proliferate gold necklaces, just a clanking set of metal Army dog tags on a chain around his neck.

After we shook hands I said, "You've got a very nice house."

"Belongs to friends of Lissta's," RB replied. "Hey, Lissta," he yelled down the staircase, "would you mind bringing us some of that coffee? Lissta? The good beans."

She replied with a sultry, "yeah," through the intercom speaker on the wall.

I followed him into the photo gallery.

The photos were his last nine years, time trapped in color and black-and-white. He'd worked Bosnia, Sierra Leone, southern Lebanon, south Sudan, Kosovo, East Timor, wall-to-wall tired faces, muddy weapons, broken bodies, crying children, burnt houses, charred mosques and churches.

His Desert Storm photos lined the rear wall of the room at the end of the gallery. That rear room had several large curtains suspended from the high ceiling. The curtains could drop and hide the photographs or fall across the open area and reconfigure the space. Three batteries of lights and two reflectors sat in the room; obviously he could use the area as a studio. A door leading to his photo lab was on the north wall.

I looked at the Desert Storm photos. Young faces peered from tents, men stood in chow lines, specialists turned screws on radios, a tank crew tightened track and laughed. "The shower," RB snickered. I looked at the black-and-white: Sergeant Benski stood beneath an oil drum suspended by chain from an A-frame, water draining from holes in the drum, a wet T-shirt dropped in front of his crotch. "These're from December '90 and January '91." He showed me a series of photos, tanks on line as we prepped for the attack, tanks maneuvering, superb action photos. "And here's the day we attacked." The photo showed me standing on top of the CO's tank, scarf on my neck, goggles up on my CVC helmet.

"Desert Storm did me good. These photos got me my first assignment after I left the Army."

"I look grim," I remarked. I pointed to the picture of me on top of the tank turret.

"You look *sharp*. Hands on your hips, and your jaw. Strong jaw."

The next photo series showed tanks rolling through sand berms—though stills, each photo had the momentum, the pulse of attack. One photo captured a magnificent wall of dust, grit kicked up by a tank company, the dust wall like boiling brown smoke, the writhing muscles of an immense brown animal.

"*Time* bought that," RB said. "Didn't use it, but they bought it."

On the wall by the door to his lab he had two framed photos of blown-out Iraqi tanks. On the door itself was a framed photo of two dead Iraqi infantryman, crumpled legs-to-chin within a bullet-punched truck.

"You know who killed those men?"

"No."

"*We* did. You gave the order, Ben pulled the coax trigger, I fed the ammo. Ward's sittin' down in his driver's seat pissin' his pants."

"Is that the firefight after the war was over?"

"Yeah. . . . But it ain't over, we know that. We still got Air Force bombing shit in Iraq every day. Like we got GIs still in the Balkans who were gonna be home four years ago." Guyton's eyes were wide, bright, liquid. "This tee-vee reporter interviews me, ast me if that picture's a trophy, like a moose head with antlers? Woman *said* that—like my photo's a stuffed moose? Shit. I don't put it up 'cause I'm proud."

To the right of the door: My eyes fixed on the only picture of the burning Shia village he had on display. The photo showed smoke pouring from thatch, an Iraqi wheeled infantry carrier between two huts. Next to that photo was the comic relief—a picture of me with my tongue out, a grinning medic daubing my tongue with a swab. Beyond the comic relief: an absolutely stunning photograph of the Arab kid who escaped the massacre, the muscular, rumpled boy standing on a knoll above the riverbank, the Red Cross on the side of the medic carrier his near background, the suggestion of white-blue sky and brown desert beyond, the boy's tousled black curls on his neck like the jaunty locks of a smart teen rock star, but his lips hardened, his jaw paralyzed, his two black eyes riveted on a tangible horror.

"Abdul," I said, "looking at his hometown burn."

"Exactly. It's one of my best. I hate it."

"I haven't thought about that Arab kid in a while."

"I have," RB replied as he opened the door to his lab. "We'll talk in here."

Inside his lab, a high-tech lab with a computer and view screens, RB started talking. I'll give it to you like he said it, as best as I can. He said a lot because he had so much. The man was covering nine years, seven years as a professional photographer for global news organizations, and the better part of five of those years covering war zones that attract the world's Jumpsuits and Ted Nicholsons.

"I ran into Nicholson in the Balkans, all over the Balkans. Sarajevo, Tuzla, Athens. He's a great contact, got me instant access to places tough to get to." RB went through four or five examples, of Ted putting in a word with NATO information officers, of Ted cajoling the right people or acquiring the right stamps and papers to let Guyton and occasionally a correspondent tag along on interesting missions. "Pudge. He told me to call him Pudge. He said everybody calls him Pudge."

"I didn't call him Pudge."

"Me neither. It was either Ted or Colonel. I say this. He didn't play quid pro with me. Didn't ast me to tell him who I seen, what I seen, no debrief games. Intel types usually fuckin' with you, screw with the working press, put you in an ethical bind, you know. Stoopid public affairs, offerin' this, takin' away that. But not Colonel Nicholson, not him . . . I had to respect that."

"But he knows you'd spit in his face if he tried something like that."

RB nodded. "Still . . . we end up talking. He was smooth like that. Dig without digging."

Label that Phase One of the photographer's story. RB

established that from 1994 on he was encountering Ted on a frequent, if unpredictable basis.

The coffee arrived, in a silver pot, two huge white ceramic mugs on the tray. I sniffed it. Had to be arabica. Lissta put the pot on the table and left. Yes, he'd finished with Phase One. As I poured out two cups, black, RB pulled out the first of several photo files.

"Now, this thing with Nicholson—the Great Balkan Floating Poker Game? You know he played cards? I play cards."

"You're good," I said.

Guyton cracked a grin. "Nicholson's game, I'm in his area, I had to play. But I tell you, those poker games, *that* was access you cain't believe." He scattered several photos on the table. "President of Bosnia, the Muslim one. Next to him's the Russian paratroop commander, one in Bosnia." He tossed out another photo. "Know who that is? Right, Deputy Secretary of State. Egocentric asshole and still thinks he can play seven card stud."

"Who wiped him out?"

"Nicholson," Guyton shrugged. "Ted play some cards. I won enough to stay even, little ahead. Most everybody else, their money's Ted's. Or this dude's. He shows up two, three times in Sarajevo. Didn't want his picture took, but, that's why God made midget cameras." RB swiveled in his chair, punched the computer keyboard, spent a moment with the computer mouse. A photo appeared on the computer screen and on one of the larger viewing screens. "Nice tech, huh?" RB muttered.

"*Who* is he?"

"Easy, man . . . Bulgarian Turk name of Nilo. *Nom*

de guerre. Lemme get rid of the graininess." RB tapped the computer key and the image re-formed.

Nilo wore a greasy brown leather jacket, had a long jaw, beady black eyes, a thick black mustache, gray flecks in curling black hair. He held a shaky cigarette between his thumb and finger, and hunched forward, staring down the table.

"What's he looking at?" I asked.

"His future. Two queens and a jack."

I didn't see Jumpsuit in his face. "So who is he?"

RB didn't grin. "He's a guy around."

"Greek or Turk intelligence?"

"Pete . . . I've discovered another outfit I call Nicholson Intelligence."

Let's say the mention of Nicholson Intelligence concludes Phase Two of Guyton's story. I poured more hot coffee as he rummaged through a manila folder.

Phase Three began with, "You see I'm on Nicholson's list, okay? Man knows how to reach me, man knows how to talk to me. Two years ago, Lissta and I move in here, Paris as a base of operations, and rent free." He sipped coffee, cocked his head. "You might dig these friends of hers. Cash-heavy bohemian screwballs."

"I want to meet Jumpsuit."

"Shit. You think you do. Anyway, now, about eighteen months ago, he shows up, Colonel Nicholson, here, this French woman with him. She wants me to get on a story in Africa, in Congo, Zaire Congo . . . You want more coffee? I get some."

"I'm fine."

"No jet lag?"

"None."

"Guess not . . ." Eyeing me, he took a sip of coffee, put the mug down. "This French lady. She supposed to be with a relief organization called Medex-Medics. Ever hear of it? No?" He flexed his eyebrows. "Well, neither had I, but there's thousands of 'em. This lady's a knock-out wearin' glasses and tryin' to look Plain Jane like a lot of the field types do. Speaks poor English, worse than my French. Nicholson vouches for her, says she's got a story and he's doing us both a favor. So I do it. I convince my editor we need to visit this lepro-sorium. We go down there, me, a guy from the AP, and Mick Jones from *Newsweek*. The story's this relief ef-fort at a town in Congo, Mbuji Mayi, good people in Hell kinda story, relief outfit working with lepers. Mbuji's not that far from the Angola border, south Congo. Place is crawling with troops, lot of troops from Zimbabwe, tribe militias loyal to Kinshasha govern-ment, more sunglasses per capita than Los Angeles. It was, in point of fact, a pirate town in the jungle. Outlaw town with an atmosphere like that town in Saudi near King Khaled Military City you took me to."

"Hafir al-Batin," I interjected.

"Right. 'Cept al-Batin, all you got was coffee with your intrigue. In Mbuji, alcohol, women, gangs of men in camouflage with subs, drugs, cheap electronics, home computers, vee fuckin' dee and AIDS. One buzzed fucker drives around with a gorilla chained to his jeep. Leprosy, supposed to be cured, right? Got a pill to control it they say, but no control of nothin' in a war zone in Africa. I hear about leprosy, but outside Mbuji, I see it. Rotten legs, people missing fingers, the disease scrape their faces off. In dee-tach-ment mode I click away." His long brown index finger clicked an imaginary camera. "You wanta see?"

"I've been to leper colonies."

"Great story. Impact photos."

"I missed the issue, RB. What about Mbuji Mayi?"

He smirked. "You ain't cool, Pete. . . . Nine years and you ain't cool."

"You're fucked up too, kid. You're still wearing dog tags."

"We were so high, weren't we, for a while?" he said. He moved the coffee mug, glanced back at me. "You know why Mbuji gets the troops?"

I nodded. "There's a huge diamond mine near there."

"Right. So everybody there *stealing* diamonds, dealing diamonds, their generals, the politicians, everybody's moving or stealing stones. Or diesel fuel and guns, and kidnapping anybody you don't like for ransom. Also a good market for secondhand electrical generators and duct tape." He struck a computer key and began flicking through a dozen photos. "Airfield outside of Mbuji Mayi. Look at the white faces, now — and a few Asian faces. Russian pilots. Ukrainian arms dealers. Belgian diamond dealers. Singapore Chinese gun salesmen. Red Chinese selling one twenty millimeter mortars from North Chinese Industries Company. Koreans selling who knows. Here, South Africans. I was told this black guy's a government minister and the white's a Boer who's a mercenary. They have a *company* that owns a *battalion*." Guyton smirked at his own military pun. "Coupla Americans here. And an important figure, a gun dealer from Virginia." Guyton tapped the computer monitor. I couldn't make out much about the large, bearded man in the photo of a half-dozen people

standing beside a stack of ammo crates. "This man—
he's a cat who pays attention, in his own peculiar way.
Notices me snappin' photos. Comes over like Junior
Bulldozer, wants my camera, wants my film, wants to
buy my *kafir* butt off or kick my fuckin' ass. That kind
of guy. I tell him I'm *Newsweek,* I'm American, and if
he don't want his face in a picture to not hang out in
shitty places. I play tough guy. But you know, you never
know about men like this, who they know, who they really are, what they do if they can roll you. Our argument
starts to get hot. Who do you think shows?"

"Ted?"

"No. *Nilo.* Out of nowhere, Nilo the Bulgarian Turk
comes up, talks to this guy, talks to me. Nilo and the
redneck walk off. Five minutes later man comes back,
gives me his card, ast me for mine. Son of a bitch apol-
ogizes." Guyton got up from the computer, picked up a
file. "I have it . . . Here, Jimmy Duke Brune."

RB tossed a black-and-white on the table with a card
attached. This photo had his face and torso. Khaki-clad
Jimmy Duke was shaggy, had a goofy tooth, looked
fifty-fifty—a fifty-year-old who could shed fifty
pounds. His company was Charlton Tactical and Preci-
sion Arms, Norfolk, Virginia.

I could guess what made a fat prick like him important: muscles, corruption, the will to kill, hazy ties to
warlords and intelligence services. He had the shape of
a CIA cowboy. CIA makes ample use of assholes like
Jimmy Duke Brune.

"Why's he important?"

"I'll get to that," RB replied, and he began Phase
Four of his story. "Let's move this on five months later,
to Tirana, Albania. The war in Kosovo's about to kick

off. Whole press corps ready, NATO gearing up to bomb Serbia. Crummy dirt, Albania. You been there? Another duct tape Oz. Pillboxes everywhere, people livin' in 'em. I mean, you drive in the countryside, pillboxes, brown concrete pillboxes, round flipped-over bowls, every field. I got a hundred photos of refugees and Gypsies living in pillboxes." He punched the computer, a photo appeared on the monitor, an emaciated little boy and a mangy black dog cuddling on top of a pillbox, the boy's leg dangling over the empty machine gun slit.

Guyton punched the mouse and a picture of a Tirana street appeared. "Afternoon, a few days before the war starts . . . This haze, from generators and cooking oil. I'm shooting this street, looking for good faces, and stepping out of a pickup truck, Ted Nicholson. He ain't in uniform, that's clue one. Clue two—who's he with?" RB punched the computer and a photo appeared. "Don't recognize him? Blowup of the face."

The face became that of Nilo.

"What's Ted doing, there in Albania, Pete?"

"Possibly running guns to the Kosovo Liberation Army, or facilitating that," I suggested.

"Think so? I think so. I ain't gonna blow *his* show, but I say hello. He's relaxed, in his Pudge character. We end up talking in a bar. I say to Nicholson, you know Colonel, bet you could tip me onto a story on running guns. Ted says it's all been done, ain't nothin' new to say. Nilo don't say shit. Eyes get beady. So, I drop it. But that night, a rainy night. It was a dark and stormy night in Tirana, Albania. I'm asleep in this flop hotel and there's a knock on the door. I'm sharin' the room with four other reporters, but this dark night, they're all elsewhere, tryin' to find out about the killing going on

over in Kosovo. I get worried. I know about kidnap
gangs. I ast who it is. He says it's Ted. I open the door
and Ted Nicholson's there bleeding, got a cut on his
face. I ast him. He says don't ast, but have you got a first
aid kit? I do. I start to work on him. As I'm working on
him he says, "Remember the murders at the river, those
pix you took?" Shit, I tell him, who forgets that? Get me
copies of those photos, he says. I say I got 'em in Paris.
He says, okay, when can you get me copies? I tell him
after this goofy war. Okay, he nods. So I need to know
where I send them. He thinks and says don't send them.
I still got a set of the photos, he says, but I want a
blowup, a blowup of Jumpsuit's face. He says he'll contact me when he's in a place to get it. After I get *his* face
fixed he stands up and says, "Nilo's gonna talk to you
about gunrunning, after this war. You'll have to be cool
and let me do the advance work. Your reporter'll have
to be cool." Boom, he's gone, into the rain. Next day
I'm up to my ass in a trip to the border. Day after that
they bomb in Belgrade."

"So when does Ted get the photo of Jumpsuit?"

"Next thing I hear, I get mail from him, cryptic snail
mail. He wants me to send him the photo care of the
U.S. embassy in Uganda. That'd be July of last year,
'cause I'm back in Paris from Kosovo, only here two
weeks. I send the photo. The rest of last summer it's
down to Sierra Leone and over to Turkey. I go to the
usual bad places, but I don't run into anyone we know.
I run into more people we don't want to know." Guyton
turned in his chair and stretched. "Shoot. You want
more coffee? Some wine? Lissta buys *amazing* bur-
gundies."

"I'll pass."

"I need some more coffee," he said as he stood. "And take a big pee."

Phase Five began on the walk to the john just outside the gallery. As we left the first gallery room RB said, "These photos here, Sierra Leone and Liberia. The ones on the bottom row I took last summer. This one, town of Lunsar. Check the shots of people chopped with machetes."

I stopped and looked. They were in color and they were gruesome.

Before he closed the door to the water closet RB turned and said, "Some of those people, who got macheted. It's diamonds, men after their diamonds. Group in Sierra Leone called the Revolutionary United Front. They come into a village, cut off a man's hand, say they'll cut off more unless the villagers cough up diamonds they find in the rivers. They kidnap people for spare change, occasionally, anybody they think's got money."

Guyton did his business. He came out, I did mine. I heard him shout downstairs to Lissta for more coffee.

I found him in the second gallery. He pointed to a picture on the wall. "Here—this from a trip I made to Vietnam four years ago. It's Ho Chi Minh City. 'Cept Jimmy Duke Brune call it Saigon. He knew the street."

"Brune saw this photo?"

"Standing where you're standing. Brune come through Paris, calls me from his hotel. He's my Congo buddy now, big bullshitting redneck act. You can tell he's drinking, hear his gills pop over the phone. Wants me to meet him in a café. I say I'm pretty bizzy. Says he read an article on me about my photos in my gallery. Says he bought a book of my photos. I say no shit. He

says he wants to come over and see me, have me auto-
graph the book. I tell him France is a free country, sort
of."

"Was the book *Neutral Density*?"

"Yeah . . . You know about that?" Guyton's chest
puffed out just enough.

"I read about it on the Internet."

Guyton nodded. "So did Jimmy Duke Brune. Anyway, he toodles over here, chick in each arm, *nommes* of
Neriah and Suze. Both these whores fat, wear chains of
rhinestones, chokers, man, necklace like a lasso of fake
ice. We get the man's taste? Fake diamonds and big leg
women."

"Does he have the book?"

"Yeah, he's got it. He's got two copies. I'm touched.
He gotta see my gallery. Lissta's suspicious but shit,
he's got two books. Lissta's dogging 'em up here with
me. Lissta's wearing a workout suit, so everybody sees
she pumps iron. She crosses her arms, pouts like a cop,
bad. Up here, at first Jimmy Duke's goo-goo over the
photos, still the happy drunk. But once we move to
Congo photos he starts asking me about Nicholson.
'Cept he call Ted 'Niggleson.' "

"You're no longer flattered?"

"Actually, I'm floored by his women. I gotta try and
shoot these babes. I mean, the architecture." He brought
his hands up to his flat, naked chest. "The light, so
bright in all these rhinestones. And the women—bul-
bous."

"What'd he ask you about Nicholson?"

"I ast him how he knows I know Nicholson? I figure
'cause Nilo tole him. No, he heard of me through a card

game in Kampala. Jimmy Duke lost eleven thousand bucks to Ted."

"You're kidding."

"Well, that is a big pot for Ted . . . But maybe he's playing for a bigger pot?" We were in at the entrance to the rear room of the gallery. RB scratched his chin. "Jimmy Duke tells me Ted says he'll forgive the debt, but he needs some info."

"Why's this gunrunner tell you this?" I asked.

"Pete—standing in this room, Jimmy Duke pulls out a copy of the Jumpsuit photo, the blowup? He says, 'I hear you took this, Guyton.' See, Nicholson ast him, ast Brune if he's seen this guy. Jimmy Duke says he don't trust Niggleson for dawg squat. Now, the egg-zack *reason* for distrust, that's shady, but—well, I tell you how *he* said it. 'Nicholson, see' Jimmy Duke says, 'Niggleson, man, like he's *too* much around. You, Guyton, *you* show the fuckin' truth. I looked at your book, Guyton, I seen your photographs. Man, you been out friggin' there and you showin' the *truth.*'" RB paused, his hands in the pockets of his pants. "That's an exact quote. . . . Does what he say to me, why he talks to me make sense now?"

I nodded.

"Didn't expect wrasslin' with truth out of that redneck gun smuggler did you, Pete? Huh?"

"No . . . So why was he flattering you?"

"Flatter me? Setting me up? Funky drunk redneck with two fat whores?" He laughed. "Man, sometime *you* gotta be there, huh, Ford." Guyton shook his head at me. "I see a cowboy squeezed for eleven thousand, but also a man who knows his own ass—and maybe some of his soul?"

"Okay, let's say he's real."

"Naw, don't have to go that far, 'cause he is deep-dyed bullshit. Somethin's eating at the man, Pete. Saw some of it when he looked at the Saigon photograph. Then he looks at the Sierra Leone stuff, the armless, the macheted people. He gets more peed. He starts into something like he expected me to know something I didn't. 'That's Lunsar,' he says, pointing at this photo, here, this guy with the cut-off foot. And Brune's eyes narrow, a fraction, that look a hard guy gets, 'cept the look is his whole body. Shoot, I'm thinking, gimme a camera for this face. Then he says, 'Thass Mr. Oliver territory, man, you know? Lunsar. Nicholson and fuck-ing Mr. Oliver. Nicholson introduced me to Oliver.' I say, Jimmy Duke, *who* is Mister Oliver? 'That village, this one, Nitta-something, near Kono. I been in there. I seen Mr. Oliver there. Diamond dealer. Now the fucker thinks he wants me outta business. Shid. Think fuckin' again.' Now I'm thinking, that's a pretty strange thing for even a drunk redneck to fix on. The character keeps starin' at the photo, then starts repeating himself. 'I been in that village. I been in that village. Nitta-what? Shit. I *been* out there.' Thass what he says." RB pointed into the rear room, walked into it. He wanted me to follow, so I followed him. Guyton stood beside a bank of lights, the silvered umbrella reflector behind him. "Then we slide in here, Brune and me, standing right in this spot. The whores are sitting on big pillows I had in here at the time, Persian things. Jimmy Duke looks square at this photo, the one of Abdul. He says 'And damn, I seen *him,* too. You got all the members of the fuggin' Nig-gleson Network? Shid, Ali. All you guys meet in the goddamn desert?' Brune's laughing now, his face bright.

He gets something I don't, he gets what's hidden in this Nicholson world, I mean. I can see it in his eyes, the man's got a Who's Who. So, I say who's Ali? He says 'Ali moves guns from the Czech Republic, with your pal Nilo. Works that bridge crew.' Then Brune bites his damn big lips, put his huge red eyes up close to the photo. 'Yeah. Shid . . .' Then his voice goes soft. 'Hey, Guyton . . . What's Ali starin' at like that? Like he lost his mama.' That's what Brune ast me."

"Did you tell him?"

"I tole him. About the river. About all of it. I told him, 'Jimmy Duke, the man did lose his mama.' He got a sweat when I told him about it, the shootings. His face turned cherry. . . . Never know what eats at people, even a jerk like Jimmy Duke Brune."

"Then what happened?"

"He ast me if somebody did one thing good if that's right enough?"

"Right enough for what?"

"He don't answer. Heaven, Hell, nothin', he don't answer. He got real silent, went back over to the Vietnam photos. You had to let him alone. So I let him alone. I got a camera and started shooting pictures of his women, sitting on the Persian pillows. They end up stripping."

"You're kidding."

"Naw, this is Paris."

We returned to the lab. Guyton sat down at the computer, clicked the mouse. Two nude grotesques in the flesh, rhinestones on their necks, over nips, rhinestone brooches in bouffant blonde and black hair. Guyton clicked the mouse. New photo: Jimmy Duke Brune joined the girls.

"He got over his moment of aloneness," Guyton said drily.

Next photo, Jimmy Duke Brune in his jock strap, Suze and Neriah on either side. Next photo, three nude grotesques in the flesh, Jimmy Duke with a rhinestone necklace in his mouth, his fat belly and spread legs, the women clinging to him.

"Kinky," I said.

"He ordered five copies," RB replied. "Now, fore you ast where's he at, Jimmy Duke got killed two months ago when a plane of his crashed in Sierra Leone, near Kono, the diamond fields. . . . Plane had flown up to Sierra Leone from Angola. So I heard—from Nicholson. Ted told me about it. Phoned me a week after it happened. Said he played some more cards with Jimmy Duke and Jimmy Duke mentioned he'd met me. Odd call, really. Nicholson thought it might be a tip for a story for somebody, wire services maybe."

"Nicholson dropped it as a story, huh?" For a second, I felt a hot prickling heat. I licked my lips and asked, "Was the plane bombed?"

"Dunno," RB replied. "I try, can't turn up no other information. But who investigates when a slimeball gunrunner dies in a sewer?"

The phone in the lab rang, an editor from New York. "I got to take this," RB said.

He kept taking it.

I sat there, thinking. Guyton kept talking. I left the lab, wandered into the photo gallery.

I went over the details (that's what I did), as Guyton talked I went over every detail, the whole tangle, and though I knew all the faces—for they are there, aren't they, aren't they all there, on the walls, framed?—I'm lost, overwhelmed by the alleys and sewers and the savage grotesques of Nicholson's planet Earth, one corner after dark corner, here, there, over there, a maze of depravity, an absorbing depravity, a maze like Nicholson, oddly built, parts that fit wrong. The details—my face flushed, that needle heat again, like I was in an airless room. I went to the john, splashed water on my cheeks and hands.

When Guyton got off the phone Lissta came in and said she was hungry. Guyton said he was hungry. Me? What could I say? "I need some air," I said.

Guyton put on a shirt, put his vest on over the shirt. We went out to a café.

We didn't talk at all. I'm thinking, like thinking's my punishment. Lissta watched me as she chewed her salad. In the half-light of the café her eyes shone like black diamonds. A Paris evening, the wonderful lights, the gray stones, the shadows: I have to wait and think and in a compressed, stifled fashion feel what Nicholson lived and Guyton put together piece by ill-fitting piece.

Phase Six began on the walk home.

"Do you have a photo of the woman from the Medex organization?" I asked.

"You been thinking about her?"

"You got a photo of everybody else."

"You think so? You make it sound like an accusation."

I said, "Yeah . . . I'm sorry."

"S'okay . . . I did run into her when we flew into Congo, through Kinshasha. She was in Kinshasha, the capital. Didn't get a photo."

"Describe her."

"Brown hair, brown eyes, great figure . . . I tried to get ahold of her, or Mick Jones did, when we got back to London. He tried from back in the States. Her own organization couldn't reach her."

"That trouble you?"

We were standing on a street corner. A taxi passed. He nodded. The taxi came to a sudden stop, the driver eyeing us. Lissta shook her head and the driver moved on.

As we crossed the avenue I asked "What did she say her name was?"

"A lovely name. Ariana Guillaume."

"You have an address for Medex?"

"Yeah, here in Paris. I went by there. They said Madame Guillaume was out of the country and they had no information."

"That disturb you?"

". . . You know, Ford, you ain't the only pro on this street."

I grinned and he saw the grin. "You agree there's a possibility Ted was doing a favor for a French intelligence agent?" I asked.

He shot me a glance, slightly bemused. "Like, helping get a reporter on a story the French wanted to get international play, for whatever reason? . . . Yeah, it's possible . . . If that's the case it was done smooth. And she's some intelligence agent."

He gave me the address for Medex-Medics.

PHASE EIGHT, JUMPING AHEAD OF PHASE SEVEN: AS we passed the kiosk advertising the Bosnian rock band I said, "You saw Nicholson last week."

"We both did," Lissta replied, cracking her chewing gum.

"They had a disagreement," RB said coolly. "Lissta don't like pistols."

"I like the diamonds, Robbie." She shrugged.

Guyton read my reaction. "Lemme get there," he said.

PHASE SEVEN, BY FORCE OF WILL, STUCK BACK BEfore Phase Eight.

In Guyton's lab, an open bottle of a liquid silk medoc Lissta took from a rack in the basement.

Over Guyton's shoulder, at the computer, I looked at the screen and asked, "Abdul on the bridge in Prague?"

"Richer than that. Remember what Jimmy Duke said about Nicholson's man, Ali? I keep thinking I'm going to hear from Nicholson on the gunrunning story. Early February, a travel magazine ast me to do something for them. I suggest 'Romantic Prague, in winter.' The editors snap to that. Midmonth, Lissta and I fly to Prague. Prague photo essays, at least for slick travel magazines, always the castle and the Charles Bridge over the Moldau River. You got to see how this is, visually." Guyton punched a computer key, gave the monitor a squint. "Bright, chilly day, perfect for the kind of crisp definition I want." A medieval bridge appeared on the screen, with statues of bishops and kings, the old-time warlords, lining the sides of the span. People covered every square centimeter of the bridge, joggers in hot neon colors amid black leather jackets, teens in heavy coats, bearded swarthy men (Georgians, Azeris, Arabs) in gray overcoats and shabby military motley. "Cold day and a wall-to-wall crowd. People, folks hawking stuff on the bridge. I have a day. These faces, condensing breath, like the wisps of air over the river, where it ain't ice. I get that kind of place-and-people balance, river breathing and people breathing. See." Guyton ran through several photos, men peddling phony Orthodox icons and Cold War leftovers of the Soviet Army, Soviet Army hats and helmets, Stalin medals, miscellaneous Warsaw Pact uniforms, gas masks, and knives. "Now, I hear the Czechs forced these folks off the bridge back in 1995, too much dope, but look, here they are. This guy, Vlad. I get to talking to him." A shaggy blond-headed man with a blond beard, blue jeans and garrison green Soviet Army jacket appeared on the screen. "Vlad said rumor had it you could still buy a Russian tank or field howitzer if you had the hard currency, from jokers hanging around there. Lotta Yugoslav stuff available, too."

"Where's Abdul?"

"Hey, my eyes are open. I'm working and my eyes are open. We're there three days, all good days. Finally, we're buying Vlad a cup of coffee in a café. We've gotten palsey like I hoped. In the café I show him a photo of Abdul's face, a blowup. I say, 'You seen this guy around? Maybe goes by Ali?' Vlad right there has a cow. Big time, man, Vlad says, he's big time. Asts me where do I know Ali? Am I a cop? Vlad said he don't peg me for a cop. I say one of my reporter friends is working on a story on gun smuggling. I'm checking on background for him, so don't go to pieces. If you see him, and you want to let me know, call me. You don't want to, nothing to it. But I'm gonna tell my reporter it's true, this guy's connected, right? See, I'm smooth. Vlad

nods. Vlad trusts me. He says this guy Ali. Word is he's
with an organization that sends guns all over, Arabia,
Africa. That's the word. Then he shuts up. I buy the man
more coffee. When we split I toss the guy ten bucks
U.S. and my card for here in Paris. I say, thanks, good
meeting you. You keep that card for yourself. That it for
Vlad, right? Wrong. Next day, we're planning on leaving. Bad day, anyway, icky, raining, low ceiling. Our
hotel, Vlad shows up, waiting on the sidewalk. He's
nervy, asts me to follow him around the corner. I follow
him. He asts me if I got money and time for a taxi. Me,
I say, I got a rental car. Even better, Vlad says. Then he
says, can I get a hundred dollars for this? I say, I don't
buy information, I ain't a cop, I ain't Mafia. Vlad thinks
about it, says, okay, he respects that. Lissta drives, he
rides shotgun, I'm in the back with my camera. We
drive thirty kicks out of town. We stop on a one-lane
road in the woods. It's spooky, like I'm in a fairy tale. A
spire, not like a church, but it's pointed, you can see it
across this valley, between two hills. Vlad says, There's
a brewery over there. There's some big shit in it, I hear.
These two skinheads, Klix and Bargo. They fucked up
and killed this Gypsy I know. Vlad's bitter, says it
through his teeth. Skinheads, I ast, like Nazis? *Da,* Vlad
says. Fascists. He spits that word out, *Fascists.* I ast
him, does Ali work with these creeps? That he don't
know. Ali, he'd seen Ali one time, and that one time,
he's in Prague, at this beer hall and there's also Klix and
Bargo." Guyton moved the mouse, found the photo. A
brick tower, poking from a cold, green conifer forest,
dreary, low gray clouds. The mouse moved, Guyton
tapped it, another photo appeared, this one of a very
drab but fairly large two-story house. "On the way back

we go by this place, suburb of Da-vetchy, Prague. Nice
suburb, for Prague. Vlad has us slow down, points out
this house, says a big shot who knows Ali's lived there.
House is all shut up looking, like you see. Vlad wants
me to drop him off outside a subway station. He doesn't
want to be seen coming back with me and Lissta. Says
everything he tells me's secret squirrel from him. But
Klix and Bargo, he hopes somebody takes them out.
Maybe my reporter friend can get the cops."

"What'd they do to the Gypsy?"

"Vlad isn't too specific. The skinheads, though, he
said they like boot and knife work." Guyton looked at
me. "I gave Vlad a hundred bucks."

"You charge it to the travel magazine?"

"Yeah."

I LOOKED UP AT LISSTA. SHE PUT A PISTOL ON THE
table, a small black automatic.

Call this Phase Eight and the finish.

"Nicholson's?"

"He gave it to me," RB said.

I picked up the pistol. It looked like the PPK nine
millimeter short sold in the U.S., but it had no serial
number, no markings other than the Walther name. I'm
not an expert, what I know I pick up from experts, but
I've range-fired the 7.65 millimeter European version
PPK. This pistol felt light for a nine millimeter. I pulled
out the magazine. The magazine held seven rounds,
nine millimeter shorts.

Lissta's voice had a razor lace of sarcasm. "A pistol
with no *detectable* serial number?"

"Could be a composite of several different weapons," I said. "Why did he give it to you?"

"In case I need it," Guyton replied. "See, this is where you come in again."

Guyton waited. I nodded.

GUYTON SAID NICHOLSON HAD SHOWED UP TEN days ago, at two A.M. in the morning pounding on the front door. "He wasn't himself. He wasn't smooth, he wasn't cool. Big nose there, shaking, but no big and confident personality." Guyton told me he wished he'd taped or filmed what happened, got all of what Nicholson did and how he said it. "I mean, you need to, so you can see the man, get the whole effect, like he's losing pieces. So you can hear it right."

"You talked up here?"

"No. Downstairs, inside the door. He was in a hurry, see. Ted started out crazy, like a conversation had already been going on ten minutes. He says, 'I know you met Vlad, right? Well, you gotta watch your ass for a few days, 'til it gets cool. They *may* think you're out there with me, see? Shit, Guyton, showing Ali's picture to that Russian punk. You can't do that out there.' Ted's worried, those eyebrows of his pressing down, like clamps on his face. He says, 'But just a few days, 'til we clear them out or they get out. Finally, I'm going to nail the man.' Who, I ast. Ted reacts, surprised, then makes me swear, like fuckin' Tom Sawyer. Says the man's name is Moshid. Moshid, he's Jumpsuit. Says he's learned who the woman was, the nurse out there. Then he pulls out this pistol. 'Now, this beaut's yours for the next couple of weeks. Help cover your ass out there.' He said that."

"What'd you say?"

"Nothing. I'm shook."

"What'd you say?" I asked Lissta.

"What do you say, stud?" she retorted. "A frightened man grins and gives you a pistol?" She pulled the wad of gum from her mouth and tossed it in a trash can. "It was a phony grin. The only thing real was the sweat on his face. And the pistol."

"So where do I come in?"

"I can't do it like he did it," Guyton replied. "Ted talked fast, I mean, like a guy doing the end of a car ad, speed talking, tax, title and license. Takes me longer to think it than he said it."

"Just spill it."

"He's talking something about you and your fucking theory of the crime, how he's amazed you had so much of it nine years ago and how bit by bit out there—he kept saying out there, out there where he is—bit by bit he picks up the concrete. He says all this and it makes a crazy sense, like he's simultaneously proud of you and mad with you, more mad with you than he is Jumpsuit. He said you shoulda been out there too instead of getting rich."

"No."

"Yes. Which makes the rest of what he said fit into a kind of logic."

"Bull," Lissta interrupted. "He used you, Robbie. . . . And he really used you, stud."

"I said a kind of logic," RB mumbled.

Lissta stared at him as she stuck a fresh stick of gum on her tongue.

I spun my hand, angrily. "Give it to me."

"He said he'd had the word out this rich guy Pete Ford was financing a hit on Moshid, like a Mob contract, a hit to take place in Europe. In Europe, he kept saying Europe. You're in it with somebody named Sam, an Arab named Sam."

"Samir?"

"Samir. He's got a rug business that covers drugs and weapons, in Istanbul. He said to tell you it was just to smoke Moshid, something he improvised when the shit went down in Prague. He said to give you a heads-up but it'll be okay, he's out there. He'll tell the rug dealer. And that's when he grabbed me. Colonel Nicholson grabs me." Guyton stared at me, hard. "I didn't realize that old man was so fuckin' strong. But I can feel this guy shaking. There is nothing smooth, no *brilliance*. 'My crew,' he says. 'I got to clear 'em, Robbie, if it doesn't work,' he says. Then, like he's suddenly aware he's grabbed me, he lets go of me, reaches into his pocket, and pulls *this* out."

Guyton had a small leather pouch in his hand. "Again, it's like another conversation he thinks we had but didn't, not quite. 'Member Jimmy Duke Brune?' he says. 'What I told you about him and his French merc friends? You never got anybody on that story, did you, 'bout the crash that killed him? Well, RB, *that's* a story.' He tosses me the pouch. 'You be the banker, like we agreed, huh? Keep these beauts. I may need 'em for short-term financing.'" Guyton opened the pouch, dumped three large, uncut diamonds on his palm. "You want to look? They ain't paste like Jimmy Duke had on his whores."

I looked. They were large stones, huge stones, figure each one for at least ten carats of crystal carbon.

As I examined the stones RB said, "Then, that's it. It's over. Ted turns, leaves, no 'good-bye' just a crack about 'short-term financing' like he's looking for a used car. He heads down the street, starts to *run,* for God's sake, runs right into the night, and I'm standing there at the door of this fancy pad in Paris with a pistol and a sack of high-dollar diamonds. Shit. I'm thinking, I photograph too real stuff all that time that looks so fuckin' unreal when I print it, your brain rejecting what's too horrible, you know, machete slashes on babies, and then now, with Ted, I'm *living* it. I felt like, like, what do I do? When I say it was weird, it's weird, and there he was spilling all this and running, like he was on drugs. 'Cept it wasn't drugs—oh, maybe some speed, Lissta thinks it coulda been speed, maybe he was using uppers, at the pace he was keeping, here, Prague, Uganda, but he was *scared,* Pete, I felt it, I seen it, I seen that kind of scare, I capture it on film 'cause I *can* see it. He was scared and he comes here and it's spilling. All kinds of pieces he's spilling, right on my front porch. Me, be the banker? When I *ever* talk to him about a *banker?* Jimmy Duke and French mercs? I think he'd forgotten which story I was supposed to get, which set of lies, you know? What bugs me is that enough of it was true to get these diamonds, get this gun, and get him killed."

CHAPTER 10

THE NEXT MORNING, OVER AN EARLY BREAKFAST, I told Guyton I had to talk with Abdul and Nilo. Nilo, I said, he's critical. But odds are, locating Abdul and Nilo's intricate. Since Ted dropped this lie I'm financing a hit on Jumpsuit, I'll bet you five million Ted's killers aren't finished. Think Mob war — that's the analog. Abdul, Nilo, if they aren't in hiding, they will be. As for Ted's story, don't discount it as ludicrous crap. I get the impression you think his hit story was pretty far out, the way you described him? Okay, I agree, with Ted, anything's possible. But you don't believe I set up an assassination, do you? Good, I haven't. And I wouldn't, I wouldn't hire it. The contract hit's fantasy, it's Nicholson trying to pull something. However, consider who he's trying to pull. Moshid — I'm guessing by his name he's Paki or Iranian — there are facts that might sucker Moshid into assuming someone like me could, you know, fix a hit? Ted could've played that, for a reason. I don't know what reason, maybe, you make a guess, because he's desperate, trapped, trying to flush Moshid? What do I mean? I mean, the right circles in the Middle East, if Moshid knows old-timers who can tell him how CIA played games out of Beirut in the fifties, before you and I were born, bottom line, he won't dismiss a hit story as fabrication. Their minds buy conspiracy theories 'cause that's the way . . . that's the way they operate. I lived in Beirut, RB, you know that? When I was a kid. A conspiracy to commit homicide? Business as usual, standard-issue politics. Homicide's his job, RB, a job he understands. Moshid—you saw how he killed that nurse. Easy, loose, a day at the factory for a confident killer. A killer like Moshid, what he understands is other killers, which may have been Ted's angle. . . . The point is, RB—and you said it—Ted's put me back in it. If what he told you's true, *if* he put the story out I financed a contract, for whatever reason he used me and the net result's I'm involved. Now, why I know I'm nuts—I feel like thanking the son of a bitch. Like, thanks, Ted. For whatever reason, lie, manipulation, *delusion,* the net result's he's kicked my ass. I'm not sitting in an office at a desk, feeling sorry for myself, I'm not on a goddamn tank, paralyzed by the orders of idiots. I got five million bucks and I'm saying, okay, I *can,* I can *now.* . . . So here are the options. I wait in Paris, we could wait, but RB, I've waited nine years. Nilo, Abdul—you don't find them, you got to get out there where they see you. Prague's the logical place to start, work from there, Bosnia, Berlin, Antwerp. For Antwerp I'll need at least one of the diamonds.

I reached for the pot, poured a fresh slug of coffee

into my cup. I tugged at the scrag beard on my face. I didn't like the beard. The beard was going to disappear.

RB's smile wasn't much of a smile. "You, uh, *need* the pistol?" he asked.

"I'm flying," I replied, "today. Pistol'd never make it through a metal detector or bag X ray." I took a sip of coffee, eyed him. "Madam Guillaume. RB, Ted used you, too. She's . . . there's a chance the woman with Medex-Medics was a French intelligence agent named Elise Neaves. . . . Like, your description, if it's not her it's her clone. Ted did her a favor . . . and used you."

RB grimaced and scratched his neck. "Okay . . . What'd she do for him?" he asked.

I shrugged. I drained the coffee cup. The stuff was so damn rich, almost sweet, the only bite a vague trace of acid if you let it linger on your tongue.

AFTER BREAKFAST I CALLED THE MEDEX-MEDICS OF-fice on Saint Honore. No one answered. So I went over there to see the place. I got there a little after eight and was surprised to find it open. The gray-haired woman at the desk smiled and said she would see if she had a for-warding address for Madame Guillaume. She had no forwarding address, other than a post office box in Antwerp, Belgium. I got the box number.

Back at Guyton's, I phoned Hospital for Humanity headquarters in Brussels. No messages, but it'd been less than forty-eight hours since I spoke with Kilean.

At RB's insistence, Lissta had gone out and rented me an international mobile phone. We tried it and it worked.

I took a shower and shaved.

"I dug the beard," Lissta said.

"I didn't," I replied.

At the kiosk, beside the poster of the Bosnian rock band whose music now ruled Paris, I caught a cab to the airport.

I DIDN'T GO STRAIGHT TO PRAGUE. I FLEW TO ZURICH, left my bag at the Zurich airport, took a cab into the city. From a street corner I walked to a bank. The bank isn't impressive. It's located at the end of a short side street, a grim brick cul-de-sac. The building has no windows on the first floor, steel bars guard the second-story windows. The name on the brass plate outside the bank's metal door is tough to read. To get in, you stand in front of a closed-circuit camera.

This bank—my last visit was fifteen years ago. I've wanted to forget it, lose the key and let it go, let it drain away. But I can't quite forget it. I've failed. I can never quite toss the goddamned key.

I held the safe-deposit key up to the camera.

The door buzzed open. The banker in the hallway checked the key and the number. He nodded a pro nod. I followed him down to the vault. His key appeared. We went to the box, he used his key, he split.

I think of this safe-deposit box as a tomb. Now, you don't need to waste time and tell me. I know the damn thing could be a time bomb. If your old man was a big-time spy who spent the last three years of his life killing himself, trying to stuff his spilling psyche back into his head, jamming stuff into holes like Swiss banks, the metal box is a tomb. If you can't forget it and move on, the box is a time bomb.

I thumbed through the fake passports, long out of date (two for countries which no longer exist), glanced at the phony birth certificates (three of them for me, two for Mother), moved the wad of moldering Swiss francs, thirty thousand Swiss francs in notes at least twenty-five years old. An envelope's in the box, with the logo of the Hotel Cronos, Athens. There's also a water-stained bank passbook. I didn't bother with the letter, I didn't fiddle with the bank passbook. I did what made sense, given what I knew, given what I might do, what I theoretically could do. I took the pen, put the pen in my pocket, took the Swiss francs, called the banker to lock the box.

The pen from my father's safe-deposit box doesn't look like much. The effect is perfect—a cheap ball-point. Its plastic cylinder bears the name of a defunct German insurance company. The pen didn't scribble well twenty-four years ago when it was loaded with two milliliters of blue ink. Now, forget that ink trick. But here's the business. Pop the cap off and you find forty-five millimeters of metal barrel and an elegant breach capable of taking a single twenty-two caliber long rifle round. The little bitch works like the secret devil it is.

I left that bank, walked several blocks to another bank, a larger one located in a building several stories tall with lots of glass windows and a huge red sign. This bank's on a main drag and you can see people inside, through the big windows in the light. At the big bank I changed most of the Swiss francs into dollars. I also established an account, did the paperwork to move fifty thousand dollars U.S. from my account in New York to Zurich.

The Herald-Acre business day had begun in New

York, so I rang Samir, using the phone Lissta rented.
Fran answered, said Samir was in Rome. She didn't
have the name of his hotel but Samir had his mobile
phone and it ought to work in Italy. She didn't have a
phone or an address for his brother in Istanbul. I tried
Samir's mobile, let it ring ten times—no answer. I
thought several things at once. You could take the facts
and go several places. Why would Ted implicate
Samir's brother? Rugs and drugs—in Turkey that was
an old story.

I took a cab back to the airport. Before I caught the
flight to Prague I bought a pair of pocket-sized Swiss
field glasses.

IN PRAGUE I WENT TO THE BRIDGE. FOUR P.M. NO
luck on the first pass.

I walked back into Prague's Old Town, cut through a
throng of people standing around a three-man banjo
band. On a side street I spotted a coffeehouse, the first
floor of a sixteenth-century building. I had a cup of coffee, sat at a small table with two young women from
Spain.

I went back to the bridge, watched a young man test
the ballistics of three red balls. The juggler mounted a
unicycle. I watched him work his way through the
crowd. I looked at every face out there on the bridge. No
Vlad or Abdul. Well, today was a day to get a feel for
the place.

Five P.M. Why do I feel so rushed? Five-twenty,
shove this. I decided to drive out to the brewery before
it got any later. That was a mistake. The thirty-kilometer
drive took an hour and thirty minutes, fighting traffic at

first, then ten kilometers of bad country roads. As I drove a wall of clouds moved in and the day became dark gray.

The country road became a lane compressed between fields and trees. The road reached the edge of a clearing and I stopped the car. I saw a tall spire rising on the far side of a thickly wooded knoll, not a church spire, more like a tall stone tower topped with an archaic gray steel antenna something like the RKO Pictures radio beacon. I could see the road winding down the meadow then cutting between small hills, probably leading to the building with the spire.

I backed my rented Audi into what looked like an old logger's road. Once I backed in I saw it wasn't a road, not anymore. The road dead-ended in a clump of thirty or forty small pines tucked inside the forest, a tree nursery from the look of it.

I walked through the tree nursery into the forest. I listened—for dogs, for anything. Satisfied, I continued to move until I crossed a narrow forest trail. I followed the trail in the direction of the brewery. The trail intersected a small stream. I crossed the water on a log. The trail dead-ended at a fence line, a wire mesh fence two meters high. I looked for sensors and detection devices, didn't see any. I walked the fence, heading roughly to the northwest until I found the kind of spot you can work with, a small stream cutting under the fence. I crawled under. The forest was so thick you couldn't see the spire and beneath the conifers it was almost night with no moon. I knew where I wanted to go but I had to figure, if this brewery were an arms dump, that these people had decent surveillance technology, so I moved very slowly. I moved right. When I reached a clearing where you could see the entrance road and the parking area, I saw the dog. The wolfhound on the chain was still asleep, head tucked between paws. I noticed the chain was connected to a long wire, a dog run that allowed the hound to patrol the front of the brewery and the edge of the road. There were no lights on in either the main brewery building or a shuttered outlying building. There were no cars or trucks in the service area. I retraced my steps twenty meters then worked my way through the forest to get a look at the back of the brewery. The rear was a dump. The cab of an old Soviet GAZ-type heavy truck sat on cinder blocks amid a pile of wooden barrel staves and what looked like old metal oil drums. There was a pit of some sort, a sump behind the barrels. Beyond the dump I could see an extension of the parking area and what looked like a small loading dock on the far side of the brewery. In the failing light I used my field glasses, scanning the second and third stories of the brewery. Yeah, there was a cupola for a camera, on a ledge on the second floor. I could see a wire running from the box back into a window. The cupola, however, wasn't moving. If there was a camera in there it was sited to look down at someone coming out of the dump and walking into the lot by the loading dock.

A drizzle started and the gray light disappeared. In darkness I worked my way back through the woods to my car. By the time I reached my car I was soaked and sweating. It was jet black, now, with the rain and nightfall. The rain was bad. It took me almost two hours to get back to the outskirts of Prague.

In a gas station I stopped, filled up, then pulled out my city map. No, it wasn't that far. I drove up into the suburb of Devicka, down the street past the dead end where the house Vlad had shown Guyton is located. The road up there had a lot of loops and curves and no streetlights. The rain made it even tougher. At one point I got out to check a street sign and an address. When I got near the street I parked. I saw what looked like a couple of small apartment buildings over to the left. I didn't want to sit there with the headlights on. I didn't want to walk down that street, either, but I did. Soborska Street, a short road dead-ending in a field. Only two houses. The rain was so hard and it was so dark I almost walked into a car, an abandoned car with its hood up. I identified the house that had to be the one Vlad showed Guyton, a brick two-story with a high wooden fence, and didn't see a light in the place. I went back to the car, drenched, frustrated. That house seemed to be shut tight.

I tried phoning Samir again. Ten rings and no answer.

In my hotel I had a room service schnitzel and took a hot shower. I thought, you know, you got five million bucks, a ton of information, and a cold trail. I ought to give this two, three more days. Or is Rome a better bet? I could call Kilean. . . .

I toweled off, climbed in bed. I almost called Kilean. But I didn't.

CHAPTER 11

·

MORNING. RAIN ON THE WINDOWS. IN THE HOTEL
lobby I bought a large black umbrella. I went to the
bridge. Yes, the slow, miserable rain reduced the bridge
action to quick-stepping passersby. Still, I watched for
thirty minutes, because you never know. Then I thought
about going to a Prague gun club, renting a target pistol
to shoot at the club, and palming a couple of twenty-two
long rifle rounds. I returned to the hotel, but the
concierge who checked for me said the gun club didn't
open until three that afternoon. Can't wait, I decided, I
need to scope out that brewery. I decided to head for the
brewery, do the gun club that evening.

This time I didn't park in the tree nursery. I drove on
down the lane, past a huge locked gate that blocked the
drive into the brewery. The lane wandered another kilometer before it died in a tree line. It took me five min-

utes to turn the Audi around. I drove back up the lane, slowly.

I hit the brakes. The old man was locking the gate, a small white pickup truck in the road. I thought he heard me but he gave no indication. He wore a brown bowler, a short brown leather jacket, and green hunting pants. Finished with the lock, he climbed in the truck cab and drove off.

I let him disappear before I started rolling. The truck was a small Toyota, easy to follow. He was three hundred meters ahead of me when he reached the main highway, and turned left, toward Prague. I could get closer to him once the traffic began to thicken.

I followed him into Prague. The old man finally stopped in back of a concrete Stalinist monstrosity of an apartment building, an ugly one in that ghastly section of Prague's Sixth District, behind the old Hotel Internationale.

I parked. I went into the apartment building. Ugly brick, rusted, chipping metal girders. By the time I entered the building's front room he wasn't around. The doors leading into the lobby were locked. There was no doorman or concierge.

I walked past his truck. The bed was filled with a couple of dozen plastic cases containing empty beer bottles. The bottles had no label. I peered inside the cab, tried the doors. The doors were locked. I didn't see anything except a pair of black leather gloves on the seat, no papers, no cigarette packs.

Since the rain had slacked off to a drizzle, I walked across the street, waited about twenty minutes. The clouds thickened and the big drops started falling again.

I WENT BACK TO THE AUDI, HEADED FOR THE HOUSE
in Devicka, which—according to the street map—
wasn't that far from the Stalinist apartments.

The rain slowed traffic to a plod. Trying to escape a
traffic circle that was missing several critical street
signs, I ended up driving through the intersection a half-
dozen times. Finally, I made an illegal left-hand turn,
complete with spinning tires and screaming engine. The
street curved and started uphill, a long grade leaving the
city for a row of homes and houses and several cleared
lots set for new construction. In the dark last night I'd
missed the new construction. That might explain the
lack of streetlights.

The road looped through a couple of short switch-
backs I remembered. I noticed pine trees behind the
houses. The road wound through a small park, cresting
the ridge, passing a handful of buildings and a large
field with high, thick brown grass. Slowing, I caught the
street sign for Soborska Street. I stopped, peered
through the slashing wipers. The two small buildings to
the left—the ones I'd identified as apartments—had
woods behind them, heavy evergreens marking the outskirts of Prague. The buildings looked like fourplexs
and newly constructed. I noticed a new, blue Mercedes
sedan parked in the drive in front of the rear fourplex.

On Soborska Street itself. Two abandoned Moskova
cars sat in the cul-de-sac to the left, their hoods raised
and motors missing. In daylight both of the houses still
looked vacant.

I walked down the street, watching the two-story
house, the rain falling hard, a cold slop. I reached the
empty field, walked toward the tree line then angled

right to a place where I could get to the wooden fence and see into the backyard.

I saw a large dog lying on the green concrete patio behind the back door, lying flat on its side in a rain puddle. At first I thought it was the wolfhound from the brewery, it looked like it might be that big. The dog wasn't moving and in this heavy rain that made no sense unless the animal were dead. I looked around, saw no one, so I climbed the fence.

The dog lay on the concrete in a pool of rain-diluted blood, three bullet holes in the dead German shepherd's side.

The dead dog turned my stomach.

It did not look like anyone was inside, I didn't see any sign of surveillance devices or alarms—otherwise I wouldn't have done what I did. I went to the back door, grasped the knob, turned it until I knew it was unlocked. I cracked the door, listened. An open bottle of French burgundy was on the kitchen counter, a stack of books, a small black leather bag, an unusually large mobile phone or radio device on the table on the far side of the counter. A lamp burned in the next room. I entered the kitchen, glanced into the room with the lamp. It was a den with scattered books and papers, a toppled bookshelf and Nilo's body on the red carpet.

He was faceup. He wore a dirty brown leather jacket, had a big black mustache, and two bullet holes in his chest. I bent down, touched his jacket, patted his pockets, reached for his wallet.

That's when I heard the woman's muffled scream and the sound of a fight on the second floor.

I raced from the den for the kitchen and the back door, intending to get out. I'm not proud of any of this but it happened, every damn bit of it happened and if I don't have an explanation at least I have the sequence. I bolted for the kitchen door and like a dumb jerk I didn't pay attention—I felt my shoes slip in rainwater on the floor, the rain I'd brought in. My feet shot forward and I fell hard, knocking a chair to the tile floor. There was no time—too late to fiddle with the damn door. They were coming down the stairs now, several people and the sound of someone struggling. Still on my knees, I set the chair upright. Did they hear the chair fall? As I crawled behind the kitchen counter, sliding underneath the kitchen table like a four-year-old, I caught a brief glimpse of them, stumbling away from the staircase, two skinheads in black leather, one with his hand over the woman's mouth, the other at her legs clamping her knees and fighting her ankles.

With a struggle like that, they didn't hear the chair.

They staggered into the kitchen, cursing in German. The hall door banged. From beneath the table I saw legs, a woman's struggling legs and shoeless feet, kicking, flailing, and two sets of black leather motorcyclists' pants. The woman slipped, fell to the floor, her red-brown hair wild and tangled.

Her face popped up, a silver inch of duct tape slapped over her mouth. Her eyes popped double when she saw me under the table, raw shock in that split second where panic abruptly encounters the ridiculous and utterly unexpected, fear momentarily jolted by amazement.

Elise Neaves's split-second eye-popping stare—the most talented comedienne couldn't replicate it, she'd never get the adrenaline and the fear and the stark terror in those eyes, or the way her mouth jerked the tape. And the moment was over and done so fast there'd be no laughs. A black-gloved fist slammed her on the high point of a perfect cheekbone and knocked her backward against the wall.

"Get the syringe, over there," one of the men snapped in Prussian German.

Black Wehrmacht jackboots cracked the kitchen tile, turned on heels. The man was opening the black bag. "Shit, you stone fockin' moron. You godda hold her," he said.

"Fock."

Elise screamed but through the tape, mute animal.

He hit her again, pulled her off the wall.

Here I am, I thought, on my butt, watching. Move now? If they were using sodium pentothal they weren't going to kill her. I started to sit up, looked around for a weapon.

They tossed the empty plastic syringe on the floor and it bounced in front of me. A roll of silver duct tape hit the floor.

"Klix?"

"Shut up . . . The bitch. She's going . . . Okay. You gid her purse? She have the diamonds in her purse?"

"Here."

"Good. Let's go."

"Whaddabout Nilo's fockin' body?"

"Yeah, anna dog, too, man. All of it. Feed the fockin' dump backa the brewery. I'll get the car. Hey bitch. Bitch? You doozed, bay-bee? Talk to me, asshole. Fuck. Need a liddle more? . . . Gimme another syringe, there."

"Pentothal?"

"Shit . . . A fix for pussy."

You could hear them fumbling with the bag, Elise making a soft, guttural noise.

Thirty seconds passed.

"Yeah."

"Shit. Get your hand out of there."

"Man—"

"Fockin' creep. . . . Okay, stand up . . . Okay. Lift her. Shit."

They picked her up and went out the back door, into the pouring rain.

I checked the window. They were taking her toward the gate, to load her in the car from the driveway. Figure I had two minutes. I stood up, ripped through kitchen drawers. No butcher knives, no meat cleaver, only steak knives. I hadn't felt a pistol on Nilo's body. All right, steak knife.

The huge mobile phone clicked, started buzzing.

Glancing out the window, I took the big phone off the counter. Damn—a rippling matrix of small red and green lights below the mouthpiece. The mobile phone had a tiny digital attachment, a mobile encryption coding and decoding device, a digital voice scrambler. A small black diskette, probably a crypto chip, fit into a slot on the side of the phone. These punks carried sophisticated technology. The phone clicked and buzzed again. I punched the On button. The phone whirred, the crypto lights winked sequentially.

From the digital fuzz: "Klix? Bargo? Was she there?" A nervous voice, speaking English with an almost-Brit accent, a Paki cadence. "Did you find her there in the house?" How-oose. That's how he said it. "Lo? Klix?"

I'm not sure why I did it. I scratched my fingers over the mouthpiece, to simulate static, I suppose, but I didn't think it through like that. I wasn't cool. I thumbed the Off button.

My thoughts were like the crypto-code lights. A ripple of Man. God. Good God.

Good God. I put the phone on the counter.

I looked at it for a second. Good God, what an idea. What a stunt.

Yes, it was a stunt, but a stunt you can paste a reason on. I reached in my jacket pocket and grabbed my mobile phone. No, the skins hadn't returned to the backyard.

It was all I could do to punch in Samir's number. I brought the phone to my ear. Dear Lord, let's get an answer, let him answer.

Three rings and an answer.

"Are you there?" he said. I took it as calm as I could. Yes, it sounded like the same voice, the voice at the end of the crypto phone now answering on Samir's mobile.

"Samir?" I asked.

"He's not available at the moment. May I tell him who is calling?"

I had to accept it. There wasn't much room for doubt—he had to be the same man who'd called on Klix and Bargo's phone.

I could hear the blood in my head. "Tell him . . . tell Sam Pete Ford called," I said, trying to think.

"Oh yes, Mr. Ford. May I tell him where to return the call?"

I tried this. "Doesn't his phone give you my number? On the digital caller ID?"

"Why . . . yes it does. I'll have him ring you there?"

"No, don't bother him. I'll call back in a couple of hours."

"And where are you Mr. Ford?"

"My hotel, actually . . . Tell him I'll call back."

I clicked off. Maybe I clicked off too fast. Lord. Ted's stupid ploy—there were a lot of ways to get there, but apparently Moshid had Samir's phone. I had to believe that. I had to believe Samir was either dead or being tortured or—a slight chance he was involved, but that I didn't buy, not then.

My fist hit the counter. My shoe kicked one of the chairs and sent it into the wall, breaking it.

I went into the den. No, no gun on Nilo, but I found an axe by the fireplace. I heard the blood in my head and I tossed the steak knife onto the couch. The axe— damn, it had heft, it had grip. I raised it, brought it hard into the wall, felt it pierce the wood, felt that vibration. With a grunt I ripped it out of the wall.

I took a position near the window where I could just see the back door.

The next two minutes dragged. There were a lot of ways to get there, to get Moshid, to understand Samir. Though soaking wet, though the room was cool, I felt hot, flushed. I also felt scared and stupid, only the grip on that axe felt certain and secure. I saw one of them, slick bald with tattoos on his hands, stainless steel chain across the black leather jacket. I moved from the doorway, listened as he opened the kitchen door, heard him cough, heard him step into the kitchen and stomp his jackboots.

The stunt boomeranged. My cell phone started to buzz, inside my jacket.

The skinhead made decisions, fast and direct, give the bastard that. He marched straight into the den, heading for Nilo's body, drawing a pistol from his cycle jacket. The sight of the pistol, his head, big wide eyes turning toward me—I swung the blunt end of the axe, somehow I'd turned it around, I had the hammer-head forward, not the blade, and the first blow struck him high on the left shoulder, knocking him over a chair into the wall. I don't know how he kept the pistol, I do know I reacted like it was a bayonet drill, the axe head like the butt stroke. The second blow, a jab, smacked the naked side of his skull, the sick crack producing a death lurch.

The pistol fell on the couch. His pistol was a Walther PPK. My hand shook as I picked it up.

I answered the phone, my hand still shaking. I said, forcing cool, "Ford here."

"Mr. Ford? Yes, this is Tarek, whom you spoke with a few moments ago? I'm so sorry to bother you but—"

"Is Samir still indisposed?"

"Yes, yes he is. He, ah, wants to know where you are so he can meet you?"

"My hotel? He knows my hotel."

"Yes. You are at your hotel? Which hotel?"

I noticed a pair of handcuffs in a holster hooked to the dead skinhead's belt. I unclipped the cuff holster, put it in my pants pocket. I wasn't sure where to take this conversation, but I had a use for the cuffs.

"Mr. Ford? . . . Hello? Are you there?"

I walked into the kitchen, making sure the pistol was off safe. No, they must have already retrieved the dead dog because it wasn't out there. Where was the other skinhead? "Uh, yeah, I'm here. Could you call Samir, please."

"He cannot come to the phone, not at the moment."

I kept my voice light, controlled. "It's Tarek, right? Why can't you bring a mobile phone to him, Tarek?"

"I'm calling from the phone in my hotel room. . . . Yes, I shall take him his phone when his meeting ends.

Shall I have him try you in an hour? Just a moment Mr. Ford—"

I heard five seconds of static.

His bright, cherrio, phony voice punched through the noise. "Mr. Ford? Yes, he'll call in an hour."

"That should be stellar, Tarek. I'll start my stop-watch."

"Excellent, Mr. Ford. 'Til then."

Click. End of conversation.

How smooth. He'd taken a chance I didn't have a caller ID.

But Samir—I couldn't stop myself. There are a number of ways, I thought, to get *here*, some of them not so dark and loathsome, some of them perfectly acceptable . . .

As I dropped my phone into a jacket pocket, I looked back into the den. From the door you couldn't see the skinhead's body, just Nilo's. But you could see the axe. I could see the axe. Damn, I could see the axe.

I checked out the pistol—loaded, cocked, safety off—and glanced into the backyard. The second skin-head, a slightly more slender but muscular version of his deadhead pal, marched across the backyard. I stepped from the kitchen into the hall beside the stair-case.

Face and bald head flushed with anger and dripping with rain, the skinhead threw open the door. "Bargo?" he yelled, standing in the doorway. "Foggin' shithead, man, less go."

I wasn't going to risk a fight with this man. Fistfights are for Hollywood idiots. You know the way I trained for the desert. Get a distance, a good separation, stay out of their range, put them in ours, pull the trigger.

I wanted him alive so I aimed low. The Walther spat two rounds, one that caught him in the right knee, exactly where I aimed. He screamed, sprawled backward onto the patio, grasping his bloody clutter of kneecap, reaching into his cycle jacket—

I ran out the door, kicked for his jaw, caught his shoulder and spun him. The tough bastard chopped at my ankle, but I kicked again, got jaw. Rain pounding us, I grabbed his jacket collar and shoved his face into the flagstone, jerked his hands behind him, applied the handcuffs.

"Shit," he blurted.

"Who called for you on the crypto phone?" I asked him in German.

His pale face and head were contorted, completely red. A long stream of thick saliva spilled from the edge of his mouth, saliva instantly washed by the rain. "Fock," he screamed.

I hunkered on my knees, fired a bullet right past his head, the round thumping a rain puddle in the yard grass.

"Who called you on your code phone?"

"You wid the bitch?" he cried. "Fock."

"Who called you on the code phone?"

"Mo-sheed. Shit, asshole. You fock my knee."

"Who's the hostage Moshid has in Rome?"

"I'm fuggin' bleedin' man."

I fired the pistol, a bullet right above his nose. "I'm getting wet. And I don't like you. Tell me about Moshid's hostage in Rome."

"I doan know about no fock Rome."

"Where's Abdul?"

"Abdul?"

"You call him Ali?"

"Ali . . . Shit." He stopped, blinked, rain on his bald head, in his eyes. "Ali . . . at the brewery, man."

I said, "You resist and I'll kill you." He stiffened. I reached for his jacket, patted pockets, unzipped it. He had a black swastika on a gold chain around his heavily tattooed neck, tattoos like a blue net of veins and spiderwebs. A nine millimeter Glock automatic rode in a shoulder holster. I pulled his pistol, slipped it into my coat. In his jacket I found a set of keys, a switchblade, a set of brass knuckles, and, inside a small woman's change purse, four uncut diamonds, each of about six carats.

The change purse, knife, knuckles, and key chain went into my other coat pocket.

Then I asked, "Do you like to kill Turks?"

"Fock," he hissed.

I stood, kicked him in the abdomen, so hard he doubled with that new pain. Keeping my eyes on him, I slipped back inside and quickly retrieved the roll of duct tape. The rain made it tough but I wrapped him around the mouth, ankles, put a swatch over his eyes then wrapped his knee. "Stay put, Klix," I said. I went inside, found a pillow, took the pillowcase off, and put the pillowcase over Bargo's smashed head. I picked up Bargo's body, took it through the yard to the driveway. They'd parked the new, blue Mercedes in the drive, trunk to the gate. The trunk was open and I saw the dead shepherd. Except for the two wrecked cars, the street looked empty. I heaved Bargo's corpse into the trunk and glanced into the car—Elise lay in the rear seat, wet hair pasted to her head and knocked out cold. I returned to the yard. Klix lay on the grass, a half-baked duct tape mummy shivering in the rain. I thought about it before I did it, but I went and got Nilo's corpse and the axe, put them in the car trunk, closed it. My reasoning was very simple: I'd killed a man. I couldn't figure the Czech criminal police as allies in this. I also took the black doctor's bag of assorted drugs, paraphernalia and syringes and put it in the Mercedes, as well as the duct tape, the used syringe, the steak knife off the couch, and Klix's weapons. I checked Elise. She was breathing comfortably but still out cold. Who knows how much sedative they'd pumped into her. I tried one of the handcuff keys on Klix's key ring, removed the handcuffs from her wrists. Her wrists were raw and red. But I couldn't be sure, could I? Some restraint might be necessary. I put a loop of duct tape around her wrists. As I passed through the backyard I looked at Klix. He continued to shiver in the rain.

I gave the house a very quick once-over. The upstairs was completely devoid of furniture, though I did find a woman's purse with two passports, a French one in the name of Ariana Guillaume and the other German in the name of Margarete Erica Schmidt. In a closet I found a small, wheeled carry-on bag with woman's clothing and an airline ticket folder.

In the backyard I picked up the two spent Walter cartridges then I yanked Klix up by his jacket. We were both soaking wet and the rain was incessant. "We're going," I said. I could tell he was hurting. I told him if he didn't move it I'd kill his Nazi ass. He slumped into the front seat, wet, white pale, intense. He continued to bleed from the knee, but the bleed was slow.

ABOUT TEN KILOMETERS FROM THE BREWERY, JUST
beyond where the road became one lane, I pulled over
and said, "Okay, Klix, tell me about Ali."

I ripped the duct tape off his mouth.

"He's at the brewery. . . . You know the brewery?
Huh?"

"Anyone else at the brewery?"

"Naw."

"What about the old man?"

"Fockin' Jennek? . . . You know Jennek?"

"I know about Jennek," I lied.

"Shid . . . shit." He licked at his narrow, bleeding
lips. "You with her, man? Or Jennek and Kerch?"

"I'm interested in Ali."

He started to say something, stopped. His tongue
went to his lip again. "I got a joy in my pocket—help
the pain from my fockin' knee, huh?"

"There's Vicodin in your medical bag. How is that?"

"'Kay . . . 'kay . . . Fock, do it."

He watched me as I took two pills from the bag.
"Open your mouth. You bite a finger and you're dead."

He grinned, bared stained yellow teeth, then kicked
his head back, tongue out. His tongue out reminded me
of my tongue, the medics, the hydrogen peroxide. I
dropped the pills into his mouth and he swallowed
them, dry, Adam's apple bobbing.

Then he said, "Fock. Just two?"

"Shut up."

He smirked. Yeah, Klix had a pro smirk.

I didn't like the smirk but I left the duct tape off his
mouth while keeping the blind in place. Neither of us
spoke. I pulled back on to the road. You could hear the

Mercedes' chugging diesel engine, the slashing wipers, and the awful rain.

As we approached the entrance to the brewery he said, crudely, but in English, not German, "You know, you confuse me. You speak German, sound like an Arab speaking German. Little I see of you, you mebbe like an Arab. But you say okay, man, you sound American." He shifted in the seat, turned his head, like he could look at me, see through the heavy duct tape. "You American, are you? . . . You gonna say fuckin' Mo-sheed gonna cross us, man?" He laughed, queasily, a stuttering laugh. "That asshole colonel said he'd fock us."

I stopped the car. Klix tensed, his skin like white metal. I placed the Walther's barrel against Klix's temple. I asked, in English, "Who said Moshid would cross you?"

"The big asshole. Asshole American colonel."

"Nicholson?"

"Yeah . . . You with Nicholson?"

"What kind of lock's on the gate to the brewery?"

"Combination . . . We there, huh?"

"Give me the combination."

He did, and the number worked. I opened the gate, drove the Mercedes in, got out again, closed the gate but didn't lock the lock.

As I got back into the sedan Klix said, "You didn't say, man, if you wit' Nicholson."

"Tell me about Moshid, Klix. How do you know Moshid?"

"Move shit for him, you know. He's around. Fucker hates Jews, too. Mebbe he's killed a few, people says . . . So how you know Nicholson?"

"Where did you meet Moshid?"

"He met me, man."

"Where?"

"Berlin. The fock it matter?"

"Did you kill Nicholson?"

"Moshid had him, man."

"What was the diamond scam Nicholson proposed?"

Klix laughed, queasily. "Shit . . . you doan know that, huh?"

I put the Mercedes in gear, started up the muddy lane.

"Is Ali alive, Klix?"

"For me, better he is, huh?"

About fifty meters later I stopped the car. The huge, wet wolfhound was in the middle of the drive, straining at his chain, barking, baring dagger white teeth.

"Dog? Fock, runna bitch over," Klix said as he shifted in the car seat. That shaved, clean head rotated toward me, once again moving like he could see through the tape. "My hands, man, no fockin' blood."

"That's not good. Maybe we can do something about it. Who killed Nilo?"

Klix flashed his teeth. "The bitch did," he replied, jerking his head toward Elise in the rear seat.

The dog outside the window howled, long, deep, frustrated, and leaped again, its forepaws slamming the glass.

"Now, why would that woman want to kill Nilo?"

"Dunno. Maybe I can think of a reason. . . . Can we get away from the fockin' dog?"

The dog leaped, rattling the window, growled.

"Why would she kill Nilo?"

"Shit. She didn't. I did."

I turned the steering wheel, tapped the accelerator. The tires spun mud, caught traction. The car nudged off the edge of the road, skirting the huge dog, avoiding the tree line. Its jaw snapping awkwardly, the dog leaped again, muddy paws scraping the windows, its growl hoarse, disturbed. Mud streaks smeared the glass.

As I maneuvered the car, between swipes of the wiper blades I saw the white Toyota pickup parked near the rear of the brewery by a small loading dock.

"The white truck's Jennek's, right?"

"Doan know for sure, huh?"

I wasn't sure but I figured I'd have to park that far away to get beyond the dog's range.

The crypto-code phone started to buzz. I stopped the Mercedes just behind the Toyota and grasped the phone.

"This Moshid calling?"

"Fock I know. You godda phone?"

"Where's Jennek? He have one of these phones?"

Klix twisted his shoulders, awkwardly. "He by the door?"

"No one's at the door."

That's what Klix wanted to hear. He had his plan, I guess. When he'd shifted his weight and body he must have grasped the door handle. I still don't know how he did it, but the skinhead pulled that handle and pushed off the console with his feet, flipping backward out the door and rolling.

I dropped the phone and grabbed my pistol just as Jennek appeared on the loading dock waving a compact submachine gun with a fat black suppressor on the barrel. I threw open the car door, fired wildly and dived behind the sedan as he fired, his quiet, silenced burst ripping through the car's windshield, instant diamond fragments, a glass splinter slashing my arm. I lunged to my left, spun through water, mud, gravel to the rear of his truck, his next burst stitching the truck bed, smashing the empty beer bottles, ricocheting.

He must have thought he'd hit me, otherwise what he did was stupid and inane. Or maybe he was one of those thugs who's used to shooting civilians, sticking a sub in a kid's face and that's it. For thugs, bullying the weak and unarmed produces a reckless overconfidence. I crouched, took a two-hand shooting position. Jennek scrambled to the end of the short loading dock, right into my kill zone, his pink eyes blinking (yes, I saw them blink) his white hair bristling, a stiff ash brush of hair. As he swung the sub at his hip he flinched—that lost second of action which becomes eternity for its loser—and I fired, the round slamming into his mouth right at the upper lip and the second round striking his chest. I didn't see the second round hit because I did it like it's taught, shoot, move, the move a forward roll, a paratroop shoulder roll to the edge of the dock below its concrete edge.

I sprang up with the pistol aimed at the rain, to see Jennek, like a deflating gray sack, fall from the dock plop onto the hood of the Toyota.

Now I heard the screams and growl, the terrible growl. Maybe Jennek had heard screams I hadn't. Maybe that's why Jennek flinched. Perhaps Jennek saw it and that flinch was his paralysis. Dear Christ, you see it and you freeze.

Klix. I've seen bad, you know that. I couldn't tell, in that tangle, Klix from the wolfhound. The steeling horror. I fought my paralysis—I scrambled, picked up Jennek's submachine gun, a small Czech Skorpion. Dear God, it was awful. The dog had his throat and a mesh of black jacket and duct tape. Dear God, Klix's screams were mutters. I raised the Skorpion and fired a burst into the dog, aiming for the throat and head. That huge beast dropped the dead man, its maw red, teeth lined red. The look it gave me was animal disbelief, as if bees had awakened it, and now it stood upright, trying to snarl. But the burst had hit its head, struck throat, and with a wobble, it toppled onto Klix and into the wet black mud.

CHAPTER 12

SIX HOURS LATER SHE STARTED TO COME OUT OF IT. She came out slow, too pale, sweat on her brow. They had pumped a lot of chemical into her, more than sodium pentothal.

THOSE SIX HOURS WHEN SHE WAS DOPED: MANY OF my best theories died in those six hours. Illusions is a more accurate word—I spent those six hours killing my illusions. One or two died hard.

Abdul helped me kill the hard ones.

Abdul was there at the brewery, barely. He recognized me as I cut the cords around his hands. "Did you eat the honey figs?" he muttered, moving his battered lips with great difficulty, his eyes sunk in bruised orbits. The man's condition was terrible. He needed a doctor. He needed a hospital, a surgeon, but screwed up as he was he remained cool and composed. Why wouldn't he—he'd faced down worse. I gave him a couple of those pain pills. Abdul explained why a Czech hospital would attract Czech cops and that was a limiting factor, right? "Do you understand what you are in?" he asked, distanced, like a man fifty not twenty-five. I said I had an idea, a good idea, but you sure as hell need medical attention. Abdul nodded. He knew a doctor, one he and Nicholson had worked with on a deal six months earlier. The doctor was discreet, Abdul assured me.

The doctor lived in a little town about twenty klicks from Prague. But what do we do with *her,* he asked, as he told me what he knew about *her.* What she knew about Moshid's operation in Africa and the Antwerp connection might be very useful. If she were working with us that could be helpful, though someone would have to watch her. I wouldn't trust her, Abdul said. Of course, we could leave her in the brewery's cellar. Rather medieval, I replied. Abdul shrugged. She's a murderer and a fraud, he said. She's gorgeous, I added. He made no comment.

What to do with Elise became my decision, so we left Elise snoozing in the brewery office, tied in a chair just in case.

Since it was still driveable, we used Jennek's truck. As I drove we discussed what should happen with the brewery, with the weapons and ammunition stored there, especially with the nine antiaircraft missiles and the sordid collection of bodies. There was also the shot-up Mercedes.

Abdul took another pain pill. "Sir, there is the big issue of Moshid. Do you know who Moshid is?" He was succinct, got it all out in a couple of paragraphs, including Ted's long-range aim that had—in Ted's and Abdul's minds—justified their short-range crimes. And when he mentioned Africa and what Nicholson had learned of Moshid's base of operations in the upper Congo basin, and what he thought Elise might know—it was right there, in an instant. I knew what to do with the nine shoulder-fired antiaircraft missiles Klix's pals had stashed in the brewery.

Abdul listened to me, carefully, as he swallowed another pain pill. "I don't know how much time you have to execute something that audacious. Two weeks, I would think, at most, depending on what Moshid does with his supposed fifteen to twenty thousand carats. But what you suggest is plausible. It's logistically conceivable, given your connections."

Abdul with phrases like "logistically conceivable"—Christ, his English was now CIA, not BBC.

I thought he was turning it over in his mind, looking for holes in my instant proposal. But I was wrong. He was thinking about something else. He said, slightly changing the subject with a strange, uneasy irony, "I credit you with my life, Major."

"You mean saving your life—at the river?" I asked, glancing at him.

Abdul caught my glance but looked away, into the rain washing the window. He told me that Colonel Nicholson had picked him up from the Red Cross building in Dhahran. Three short days later, Abdul found himself on a plane to the United States, accompanied by a man named Mr. Oscar, a black man, a friendly man, a man who spoke Arabic like a Yemeni. In America, Abdul said, drily, he'd finished high school in Virginia, with the other kids calling him Doolie and his last name

Smith. Abdul Smith. Who'd believe that? His battered lisp puckered into a grin when he said he'd played a little American football, at middle linebacker, but his best sport was swimming. He'd attended college for two years in France and then one year in Cairo, establishing different names in different places. "Do you understand my situation, sir?" he asked.

I nodded. Yes, I understood.

His busted eyes clouded, two dull black pearls.

I DROPPED HIM OFF AT THE DOCTOR'S HOUSE, AT THE back door. Abdul, concussion, broken ribs, broken nose, took it from there.

I returned to the brewery. I took care of the bodies and the Mercedes, per Abdul's suggestion, the Mercedes and its contents disappearing into the chemical sump behind the brewery. I left the diamonds in Elise's change purse in the office drawer, for Abdul to pick up after he finished with the doctor. I retrieved Elise — she was still quite zonked — and brought her back to Nilo's house in Devicka. As I drove back to Prague from the brewery Abdul called me on my mobile phone. He said he was okay. The doctor was lending him a car. I knew the phone was unsecure but I gave him a couple of more details, told him to come to Devicka. When Abdul arrived I had Elise lying down on pillows on the red carpet by the fireplace, in Nilo's den where I'd found his body.

Abdul looked less clobbered. The bandage on his chin and the tape strip above his eye actually gave him a comic look, if you ignored the dark cores of his eyes. I guess we talked for an hour. I quizzed him once more about the last time he saw Nicholson. There wasn't much Abdul could add. Nicholson intended to destroy Moshid's arms deal in Europe. Africa—"Like I told you, all he told me about Africa was that we wouldn't have to worry with it," Abdul said.

"Well, we're going to worry with it," I said. I think I said it pretty hard, given Abdul's reaction. I fleshed out the operation as I saw it, told him to tell Mosoke that Mr. Ford wanted to speak personally with Major Pildi. I told him what to tell Pildi. He listened. He said he agreed with all of it, except for one thing. He asked, nodding toward Elise, "I would argue that Pildi could find out the precise location. If he did, why would we need her?"

"She'd make it easier, wouldn't she?"

"Yes . . . she could."

"Do you need money?"

"I have some access to Nicholson's."

"Anything he had would be monitored now, if not closed."

"Did I say it was in an account, Mr. Ford?"

"No."

His grin moved the bandage on his chin.

ABOUT AN HOUR AFTER HE LEFT I MADE A POT OF coffee.

I sat on the couch, next to a tray with coffee cups. I watched her breathe. The white quilt moved as she breathed.

I saw her eyes open—

Up to that moment I didn't know what I would do. Maybe we didn't need her. I did have to consider that.

I formulated two plans. The first I'll call "the Slick Trick," the other "the Direct Option." Conceptually, the Slick Trick was a smooth way to learn the critical details Elise knew about Moshid's operation and Ted's extensive mess. The Direct Option—it'd have been personally satisfying. Quite possibly a fast, direct strike at Moshid would have worked. Abdul made that case. "Shoot him in Rome, where he tried to trap you with Samir," Abdul said, "or shoot him in Africa. This is the way." No, I said, I want him tried in a court—in a war crimes court. The people he murdered—we want them named, they won't be forgotten. "Their families may not want their names publicized," Abdul replied. "My village, Saddam's men will come again, for brothers and sisters." I shook my head. No, the big payoff, Abdul, the greater good. That's how you get at Saddam. See, if Moshid's been supplying guns to the Hutu nuts in Rwanda and nuts in Sierra Leone, as Ted believed, it'll pay big to cook his vicious ass in public. If Elise has the gun-running facts, as well as the location of his diamond payoff . . . That makes nine years worth it.

But I had to figure Elise wouldn't cooperate, not immediately. Knowing what I knew about her activities and what I could surmise about her motives and aims, she'd argue and stall. That meant I'd have to slick her. To create circumstances where she thought of nailing Moshid herself, and would then work to convince me to help her pad her pocketbook, now, that's the slick trick.

To rig those circumstances, however, would require extensive deceit and manipulation. I'd have to be like her. I'd have to be like Ted. I'd have to be like Moshid. I'd have to be like Kilean and my dad.

But what a mess Ted Nicholson created. You can

make the case that Ted's mess was the result of engaging a messy world, I won't argue that. It's just you lose respect for a man when you see idealism tarnished by greed.

Take Trish as an example. Greed destroyed Trish. My hip, flaky love sold her cheesy diamonds, went from purple goop on long nails to all-business cuticles with opaque glaze. Elise—I mean, a confidence artist, a highly trained scammer. Fifteen thousand carats were the latest devil making sure she remained a ruin. But, she's also good. You can't do what she did and not be a pro. Add those knockout looks and what a work, what a talented work. See, in Elise I recognized my father, that con artist, and because of him I couldn't help but understand her. She lay by the fireplace, pale and sweating, lay there on that red carpet. A dead red carpet. You don't have this fact: Kilean told me, when he thought I could handle it, that they'd found Dad on a red carpet, in a room, in the Hotel Cronos, Athens. That's where the great Cold Warrior put a bullet through his head, shot himself in the left temple.

Now you have that fact.

So you know I don't underrate the personal cost of professional deceit.

SHE MOVED. HER EYES OPENED, GLASSY.

"Mon estomac," she said, softly.

I poured a cup of coffee.

Her eyes focused. "Coffee?"

"Why don't you start with mineral water, Elise?"

She raised her head, wiped the sweat beads off her brow. "You . . . you are . . . a table."

"I was under the table," I said.

She blinked, then her eyes shut tight as nauseous green flooded her face. "I . . . I must pee," she mumbled. She rolled to her side. I helped her stand as she fought off a wave of wooziness.

Once balanced, she pulled her arm away from mine.

"You want me to walk you to the john?"

She sighed, shook her head, walked into the hallway off the den.

TWENTY MINUTES LATER SHE HAD HER COLOR BACK. She had a tan, her skin a pale olive.

She walked into the den carrying a large, crumpled towel. She put the moist towel down in her chair. That's when she noticed her purse, on the couch. She went over and picked it up, opened it, fumbled through the junk, pulled out her lipstick and compact. She went back to the chair, put the towel in her lap, sat down, popped open the compact, scowled at herself, a pinched face in a little mirror.

As she slapped on lipstick I said, "I found your purse on the staircase."

"I remember. One of them took it."

"Is anything missing?"

"Not that I can tell . . . Why?"

"It was open, like they'd rifled it. . . . I also found your bag upstairs. It was open, clothes out of it. I put the clothes back into it. . . . I also found this." I held up her airline ticket folder. "It was on the staircase. I see you flew here from Antwerp. But you've got an interesting stub in here. You were in Rome two weeks ago, and flew there from Johannesburg, South Africa. You're jet set, Elise. Or is it Ariana Guillaume?" I put the ticket folder on the side table next to the coffeepot.

She pursed her lips, closed the compact. "Why are you here?" she asked, coolly.

"You know, you've been knocked out, six, seven hours . . . Do you want something to drink?"

"I drank some of the mineral water in the bottle in the bath. . . . Why are you here?"

"One reason I'm still here is this." From underneath the couch I pulled out Klix's mobile code phone. "I'd be very surprised if they didn't miss this. Then of course, there's you. After all the trouble they went through, I can't figure why they left you here."

She stiffened, eyes narrowing. "They took me out to the car," she said.

"Yeah . . . and about ten minutes later they brought you back inside, zonked."

Her nose wrinkled, oddly.

So I continued. "I think the man who owns this place is named Nilo. But if Nilo was the guy on the rug in this room, he may be dead. He looked like he was dead— when they dragged him outside." I took a sip of coffee, waited. She watched me through a pair of dull brown cat eyes. So I asked, "Was that man Nilo? Brown leather jacket, mustache?"

Her jaw moved, right, then left. She nodded, a curt nod, the nod flexing her delicate neck.

Now that she'd told me the truth I decided to go ahead with the con. The trick started to roll. Since greed was her thing, the con would be based on greed. "The reason I'm here, Elise, is I want my money back. It's that simple and that complicated. . . . It looks a whole hell of a lot more complicated now than when I drove into Prague yesterday. . . . Do you want to try some coffee?"

"Yes. Black."

I poured a cup for her.

I didn't say anything else. I watched her take the cup, arrange herself, put those beautiful red lips to the edge of the cup and take a quick sip.

She put the cup down on the side table. "Do you have a weapon?"

"No."

"Why are you so nonchalant? What do you expect to do when they return?"

"Hide under the kitchen table?"

She didn't smile. "You were telling me about your money," she said.

"I lent Ted Nicholson seven hundred and fifty thousand dollars, Elise."

An eyebrow arched, the arched back of a cat.

"Ted knew how to pull me. He could do that. I thought . . . well, I thought he might be covering gambling debts. His story was wild. I thought I might be getting conned a little." I shrugged, smiled.

"What did he say he wanted the money for, Peter?"

"He said he was making an arrangement to buy shoulder-fired antiaircraft missiles for a tribe in the southern Sudan. They get bombed all of the time, by Khartoum. He said it was his own enterprise, something the Department of Defense and CIA weren't touching—illegal, Elise, very illegal. But he knows I'm . . . Ted knew I'm close to several African issues. Supplying the Dinka with antiaircraft weapons protects their villages and saves lives. He also told me the money would be covered, I'd get it back." I took a sip of coffee, eyed her.

"Go on," she said.

"That's it."

"You lent him three-quarters of a million dollars . . . on his word?"

"He said that a consignment of diamonds, and I assume embargoed diamonds, would cover it. My guess, he'd get it through Ugandans in the Congo. I know that's what's going on, dealing blood diamonds. He needed cash fast and through a clean channel. You know, when Ted got killed I heard he had some diamonds. Think they were for me?"

Her fingernail ticked the side of the coffee cup. "You have that kind of cash to lend a friend?"

"Hey, I'm not rich by Wall Street standards. I mean, I had to sell what's for me a major position. I owe about a hundred grand in capital gains taxes. . . . Nicholson hurt me, financially." I scowled, twisted my face. "Hurt me personally, too. Touchy-feely stuff we oughta be too cynical for." I shook my head, took a sip of coffee.

She remained impassive. "How did you get here?"

"I've a car parked down the street."

"Ass—how did you know to get here? How did you know to come here?"

"Ted gave me the name of Nilo and this address. If something went wrong. Now, before you get any more bent, I stopped off in Paris and talked to another guy Ted knew. He knew Nilo, had played cards with him."

"Who is that?"

"Guy who was with me in the desert. He's a photographer, lives in Paris. We stay in touch. Actually, Ted told me he'd seen Bob a couple of times."

"What does Bob do?"

"He's a photographer. R. B. Guyton. Ever hear of him? He's got a great Internet site. Shoots for *Newsweek,* some for AFP, I think. Combat photographer."

"And he lives in Paris?"

"Lives well. Has an amazing place."

"Where does he live, in Paris?"

I scratched my ear, looked at the floor. "Uh . . . Rue de Bee-vray? Something like that . . . He's shook up about Ted's murder. Frankly, I'm pissed, too. . . . Are these Germans the guys that killed Ted?"

"Why would I know?"

"Well, I don't know that you would. But I've been honest with you and you haven't said anything about why you're here. It's like, you know, with you nothing extraordinary happened."

"I've been shocked at your cool reaction to the violence."

I eyed her, gave my stare a lot of velocity, then took a sip of coffee.

"How do I know," she said, leadingly, "that you aren't working with them?"

My eyes widened. "Sheesh." I put the cup on the side table. I shook my head, querulously.

"You are too calm."

"Elise, you're the intelligence officer in this room."

"I am *not* an intelligence officer."

"Right, not anymore . . ." I smiled, a winner smile. "You know, you remember what you said in Saudi, when we met? You said it'd have been better if there'd been live TV cameras at the river, when we saw the atrocities. You said international horror would've made the politicos respond. . . . I remember that. What you said was perceptive."

"You told me that over dinner in Aruba."

"I did?"

"You don't remember dinner in Aruba."

"I do. . . . Okay, I told you that in Aruba. See, I'm impressed."

"Witnessing those murders still tortures you, Peter?"

"Tortures?"

"It was war, fool."

Man, what a cold bitch, I thought. I picked up the coffee cup, then sat it down, picked up the pot and poured a fresh shot. "You want some more, Elise, or is your stomach rumbling?"

"I feel terrible," she said. "May I see that mobile phone?"

I gave her the phone.

She moved the big lumpy towel in her lap, examined the phone. "This is rather sophisticated," she said.

"Looks like it's got an encode capability."

"Yes, it does. . . . And there has been no activity the entire seven hours?"

"It rang twice, I know of."

"Did you answer?"

"No."

"You said twice you know of."

"Elise, I went and bought some coffee and milk."

"You left *me* in here, *alone?*"

"Five minutes, the store down the hill."

"Do you have *any* idea who these men are?"

"Arms dealers, drug dealers."

"And you sit here, waiting for them?"

"What are my options, Elise? I'm out around nine

hundred grand, if you include the taxes. The white knight in me would like to help nail Ted's killers, but, you know, these are the days of the bottom line. Economics trumps everything."

She laughed, a high-pitched, mean little laugh. "You think those Nazis will get you your money? Are you that stupid?"

I gave her a flush of anger. "Listen, lady. I've asked you. What are my options?"

Her eyes narrowed. "One option, my friend, is to not be so stupid. We should not be here, staying here. It makes no sense to me that they left me here. I *distinctly* remember being wrapped up in their car and the car moving. I also remember a huge dog." She shook her head, as if that would clear the gauzy memory.

"There was a dead dog in the backyard. A big German shepherd. They must've took that, too."

"*I* saw a *beast* shattering a window."

"Man . . . you had a heavy nightmare."

"I . . . I was carried through the rain to another vehicle. And"—her eyes narrowed—"*you* were there."

I grinned. "You were wet, all right. Soaked. And you were tied up, with tape and plastic ties."

Her eyes narrowed. "Where are the ties—and the used tape?"

She's too smart, I thought. Someone this smart and I'll slip up. But I had the tape and ties covered, I'd seen that possible hole in my con. The medical bag had disposable plastic ties. I'd slip one around her wrists, cut it, then throw it away. I said, "They're in the kitchen, in the wastebasket."

She rose, went into the kitchen, taking the towel with her in her arms. I sat in the couch, sipping my coffee. I was scared I'd make a mistake and this talented crook would catch on. I heard her move the trash can. She came back in, her lips tightly pursed. She plopped down in the chair again, stared at the fireplace, glanced at me, stared once again at the fireplace. She was turning over handcuffs or plastic ties in her mind.

"We can't stay here," she finally said.

"How come?"

"This . . . this doesn't make sense," she snapped, answering a question she'd asked herself, not the question I'd asked her.

"Of course it makes sense," I replied, deftly answering a question she didn't ask. "I'm out almost a million bucks. I *have* to talk to these guys."

"You're an idiot, Mr. Ford. Which confuses me, since I know damn well you are no idiot."

I gave her a perplexed stare. "Excuse me, madame. What are my options? If I want my money back?"

"You choose to sit here, with me, waiting?"

"Where would I take you? To my hotel room?"

"You've no weapons. These men are assassins."

"Okay, I lied on that." I reached under the couch, pulled out a nine millimeter Beretta I'd found in the office at the brewery. The pistol's barrel was baffled, not quite a built-in silencer but a means of reducing its sound signature. "Now, am I less of an idiot?"

"*That's* your pistol?"

"Interesting modification, isn't it? A hit man's piece." I turned the pistol in my hand, as if admiring it, then added, "I found it in here, in the corner, like it was thrown there."

"Really?"

"Yeah."

"Let me see it, please."

I paused, thinking. This was a moment to sell the con game. "Why, Elise, should *I* trust *you?*" I put the pistol on the couch, folded my fingers together. "Something's not right with you, Elise. Two passports? Two aliases? Please—what are you doing here?"

She moved her head, throwing her hair off her shoulders. She raised her chin, arrogantly.

"See," I said, feeding her a possible out, one I could work with, "it'd be easy for me to understand why you might be here if you were a French intelligence agent. Gunrunners, drug dealers, knowing Nilo, the passports—I could buy that. It'd make sense to me."

She moved the towel. From inside the wrapped towel she produced a small automatic pistol.

I flinched, and it wasn't feigned. I hadn't expected it. She must have had one stashed in the house, or knew where Nilo kept an arsenal.

She pointed the pistol at me.

"Where did you get that?"

"I've known Nilo a long time."

"Why shoot me?"

"To restore my self-respect. Toss your fucking pistol on the floor. Don't pick it up. Push it off the couch onto the floor and push it to me with your foot. Slowly."

I did as she directed.

She picked up the pistol, looked at its barrel, looked at its serial number. "This isn't Nilo's."

"I didn't say it was. I don't know whose it is. For all I know it's another one of yours."

"You're too calm, Peter."

"I don't think you want to shoot me. I've taken care of you."

"You've been such a *decent* fellow," she said, mockingly.

"Thanks . . . Please don't kill me."

"*I* must get away from here."

"What happens if the Nazis return?"

"You're dead."

"What about you?"

"I'm leaving."

"Let me take you wherever you want to go."

"What kind of transportation do you have?" she asked, almost saucily.

"A rental, an Audi, on one of those Euro excursion deals. I can take it wherever I want, as long as I drop it off in one of six semicapitalist countries."

"What kind of plates?"

Man, she's smart and thorough, I thought. I knew the answer but took my time, looking as if I were trying to remember. "You mean license plates? Swiss, maybe? I got it at the Prague airport."

Now she was rolling things around her mind, theorizing fast, a twelve-cylinder brain working all of the angles, angles I hoped I'd helped bend and direct.

I poured another two fingers worth of coffee.

"You do want a significant portion of your lost money back, don't you?"

Okay, I thought. She may have a pistol but we're back on track. I replied, with an earnest nod, "You got it."

"Have you . . . access to more cash?"

She's hooked, I thought. I replied, "A little."

"How much?"

"Now wait a second, Elise, I've already been robbed."

"How much?" Her hand gripped the small pistol more tightly and she laced a long finger around the trigger.

"A couple of hundred thousand. That's all I've got left."

"Can you get to it, here, in Prague?"

Now I dropped a key line in the con. "It'd be easier if I got it in Switzerland . . . Lucerne, specifically. I know a bank there."

She stood up, the towel falling from her lap, the Beretta in one hand, her twenty-five caliber in the other, both barrels pointed toward the floor. "Get up," she said. "If you want your money back we're leaving for Switzerland."

SHE LET ME GET MY BAG FROM THE HOTEL. THE CLERK thought checking out at eleven P.M. was oddball, but what the hell, I had a stunning woman at my shoulder.

"Elise," I said as we drove out of Prague, "you need sleep."

"You could take the pistols."

I reached beneath the Audi's dashboard and extracted Klix's Walther PPK.

She didn't move.

I put the Walther back under the dash.

She yawned.

Within ten minutes she was asleep and snoring.

CHAPTER 13

AT NOON THE NEXT DAY WE REGISTERED AT THE Hotel Metropole Suisse in Lucerne, two rooms, adjacent, both with small balconies overlooking the lake.

I pulled the dark crimson drapes across the windows, crashed into the mattress, slept until six.

I was awake, up, and shaving when she knocked on the door.

She didn't come on coy, not with those sweat streaks in her workout suit and the damp chunk of auburn brown hair falling in front of her forehead. She walked in with her hands behind her, as if looking around.

"New clothes, huh?" I said, stepping from the door back into the bathroom. "How are you feeling?"

"Super," she replied.

The outfit: a pink speed suit, nylon and a glove on her body.

Wrapped in a bathrobe bearing the hotel's logo, I

picked up my razor, started on the patch of soap beneath my chin. She folded her arms across her chest, leaned against the bathroom door, moved her hair off of her forehead.

"The gym here any good?"

"Old fat Swiss men. Stinky."

"You helped them burn a few calories. . . ."

"You're bleeding, under your chin."

I examined the nick, wiped at it with a towel.

"The Walther you showed me last night, in the car. Why didn't you have it with you inside Nilo's house?"

I grinned. "Who says I didn't?"

A calculating look crossed her face, one that worried me. She unfolded her arms. "I'm going to take my shower," she said. "I've reservations for dinner, a little place I discovered. They're picky about how men dress. Have you a tie?"

A dinner reservation. I know I looked surprised.

"Have a tie, Peter?"

"Yes."

"How many?"

"One."

"Now you have two." From the bathroom door handle she pulled a dark blue silk tie. "It's narrow, conservative. Very . . . Swiss. I'll put it on the bed next to your pants," she said. "See you in an hour?"

I SAT ON THE BED, LOOKING AT THE TIE. WHAT'S wrong? I checked my pants. Wallet, my keys in the right pocket, the Audi key still on the ring. What am I missing? The tie must have cost two hundred bucks, shimmering, pearling blue silk.

When I saw her in the lobby I began to lose control of the con. "It's on the far side of the old town," she said, adjusting the strap of the red dress with a slice down its left seam, the rip starting in the ambience of her thigh. "Let's take a taxi, shall we?"

The restaurant was quaint, all right, French, with the oddly hip name of *debutdesiecle*—all lowercase smashed together like an Internet address.

We took a table in an alcove, linen cloth, two long candles, slender wax in silver holders. I ordered a Margaux, full bottle. Her lips parted but she didn't smile. The bottle arrived. No, she didn't need to see the label. But that first glass of wine—she downed it quick, at one point several drops worth of the upscale grapes spilling over her lip. I mean, she knocked it back. Amused with herself, she mopped at the wine with a white napkin.

She was shaking me. I knew if this was going to work I had to get over that dress. Gulping wine like a thirsty farmer hitting his *plonk*, she didn't have the on-duty feel she'd had in Aruba, which was good. I wondered if I could ask her, could hint at it, start to get at what we needed to know, but it didn't seem right, her face in that soft candle brightness, wine and lipstick smeared on the white napkin. No need to rush it.

But Abdul had to know, soon. So I said, carefully, "Tomorrow, I'll get to the bank. Cash may take a couple of days. Got to sell bonds."

Elise peered into her glass of wine, took another sip. *"C'est bon,"* she said.

"You haven't given me a time frame or a plan, Elise."

"So?"

Do I ask her now? No, don't rush it. I said, "I'm putting money into a scheme I know nothing about."

"And you're not an idiot, right?"

"No, I don't think so."

"But you gave *him* a million . . ." She didn't say Ted's name. Her brown eyes saucered in the candlelight. The waiter and maître d' passed behind her.

Maybe she is on duty, I thought.

She took another sip of wine. "Peter . . . Did you kiss me when I was drugged?"

I reacted, completely indignant. *"No."*

"I remember my lips burning," she replied, taking another sip of wine.

Poof. I'd lost the con.

AT THE DOOR TO HER HOTEL ROOM SHE SAID, "THAT was a wonderful dinner."

There, face-to-face. I leaned forward to kiss her lips but she pulled her head away, turned on her heel, and skipped into her room.

BY BREAKFAST I'D REGAINED CONTROL, BREAKFAST in a room dominated by a huge girandole, a layer cake chandelier of glass pendants that couldn't help but look like thousand-carat diamonds.

As she nibbled at a croissant I said, "This morning I visit the bank. That'll start the process."

She nodded, moved the brown crumbs off her lips.

Damn her, *she's* playing with *me,* I thought.

I went to the bank by myself. I established an account, made arrangements to move eight hundred grand in cash from New York. One of my partners, Ali Smith, would be able to draw up to five hundred thousand dollars from the account. The bank officer, after I gave him the financial information and the name of my adviser in New York, said he'd have the money within four hours. I told him, "Have it take three days." He told me that I'd have to wait for four, until Monday. I said that would work.

LUNCH AT THE HOTEL, VAULTED PORTICO BY A BREEZE-way to the lake, fat old Germanoids sipping demitasses, view of the lake with a replica nineteenth-century single-stack lake steamer chugging off from the town pier. Elise sashayed in wearing a tight yellow T-shirt and faded blue jeans, California after a trip to the Laundromat.

"Did you get *my* money, Peter?"

"Monday."

She sat down at the table, perused the lunch menu.

That's when my mobile phone rang and it was Abdul. He'd been on the phone with Major Pildi. I didn't tank, the trash and phony was right there. I said, "Hey, Fran, what are you doing at work so early? It must be before six there." Abdul snapped to it. P—he called Pildi "P"—was in London. P was interested and would fly to Zurich this afternoon. Abdul would meet him there. He hadn't said anything to P except that Mr. Ford had discovered material of use to anyone with severe, vexing aircraft problems. "That's perfect Fran, go ahead and handle it that way," I said. "As long as we get it by Monday . . . Thanks . . . Yes . . . Good-bye."

"What's your phone number?" she asked.

I gave her a careful look, but flipped the phone over, read the number off to her.

She didn't write it down. "That's a French international number," she said.

I nodded. "That makes sense. I got it in Paris."

Her lips pursed, then asked, "So who's Fran?"

"Secretary from Queens. Works at my old investment firm. She knows how to speed things up, a little."

"I thought we are in the future, twenty-four-hour markets and instant borderless transfer of capital."

"Not if you invest in tax-free municipals, Elise. Small American towns and school districts are still in the paper age."

A dimple rippled in Elise's cheek. She crooked her finger at a waiter and ordered a salad.

THAT AFTERNOON: "LET'S TAKE A BOAT OUT ON THE lake, Peter."

I spent two hours rowing. She wore a broad-brimmed straw hat, a yellow sundress, and she got damned chatty, actually. The wine, again, a Chablis, and she drank it, the whole bottle, drained it, absorbed it.

At one point I tried to pry, despite the perfect moment, with the bright, crystal sunlight, the cool surface of the water, the sharp edges of distant mountains, the green of the trees. I worked the con. I said, trying for offhand, that, you know, I'd spent a lot of time in Africa, and I knew that diamonds moved around the war zones, that's why I thought Ted was a good bet to get my cash back. Then I added, without drama, "You flew to Prague from Antwerp, Elise."

She looked up from the water, removed the praying

mantis sunglasses and looked at me with disgust. "Oh, shit, Peter. Would you shut up?" She looked away, dragged her hand in the cool lake water.

ANOTHER SUAVE EVENING MEAL AT THE *DEBUTDE-siecle*.

"Let's have the Margaux again," she said.

I looked at her. The stun, man, a black dress, two thin straps on her shoulders, a bare, numbing plunge from the gold chain around her neck to the firm curve of her breasts . . .

"The Margaux, Peter. Order it again."

"You mean so you can drink the whole damn bottle by yourself?"

"What's at you?"

"You, Elise. You're taking me for every dime I've got."

"Tant pis." She signaled the sommelier, and ordered the Margaux herself.

That evening there was no wasted effort at the hotel room door.

And as I lay in bed for three hours and thought about it, I realized that was probably good.

I CALLED HER FOR BREAKFAST. SHE SAID SHE'D RATHER sleep. After breakfast I went and bought several newspapers, a couple of books.

I was in the huge room with the chandelier when my phone rang. Abdul was at most a half-hour away, Pildi in the car. Pildi wanted to talk to me in order to set his own mind at ease.

"There's a jogging path around a park, north of the hotel bordering the lake," I said. "There's a parking lot on the far side of it near a paddleboat dock and a garden with hedges cut like animals."

"I'm a green car," Abdul replied.

THIRTY MINUTES LATER, IN MY JOGGING CLOTHES, stretching at the start of the track, and here's Elise, ambling up in the pink speed suit with a sweatband on her forehead.

My first thought was: not a coincidence.

But how? Unless she was still working for French intelligence and they had monitored all mobile phone traffic and acted in twenty minutes? No, too paranoid.

"Were you going to run or walk?"

"Jog."

She started stretching. "If you're ready, go on. I'll catch up."

I started jogging on the hard-packed path. Just before the two-kilometer mark she caught me. "You're slow," she said.

"You go on, I'll catch up."

"Why don't you go faster? You look like you're in fine shape."

I saw the parking lot and the paddleboat dock through the trees to my left, through a garden of sculpted bushes, one tall and clearly a giraffe of green and yellow leaves, the wide ones a hippo and an elephant. "My heel's bothering me," I said as I slowed to a walk. "I'll sit down over there." I pointed to a bench in the trees.

"Oh." She ran ahead, yelled over her shoulder, "I'll see you on the lap."

Good, the track was at least four kilometers. At her pace, sixteen to seventeen minutes.

I sat until she was a pink blur where the track edged the lake and the boardwalk, the nineteenth-century replica steamer in the background, idle and at anchor.

I walked into the sculpted garden of wild animals, past a coiled anaconda, violets for its eyes, a rose-eyed lion, a mane of vines.

There were only seven cars in the lot. One was green, a Mercedes sedan. Abdul and Pildi stood in the dappled shadow of the elephant.

"Major Pildi."

"Mr. Ford. Your friend has presented me with a fascinating proposition." Pildi wore a blue suit and a black bowler hat, looking more precise than natty.

I laid out the idea. Twenty men, twenty good soldiers capable of an extended hike in the Congo basin. Helicopter support ideal. Silenced weapons, fancy commo gadgets, if possible. If we hit the place and he isn't there we either destroy it or we wait for him. Operational security—a fucking absolute necessity. Personal trust— if we don't have that, let's not bother. Double-crossers always get screwed, anyway."

"All right." And it was a dead serious, do-it all right. "Your Abdul has already explained. But you do not know where his place is, do you? Not precisely?"

"I'm working on that. I'm working on her."

"You sound con-fee-dahnt," Pildi said, the malarial yellow in his eyes brightening, a smile stretching his rawboned face, the scar tissue under his neck tightening.

I started to say, yes, I felt confident, but Abdul interrupted. "We don't need her, Ford," Abdul said. "Major Pildi thinks we do not need her. Tell him, Major."

But before Pildi could toss his two cents I said, "She knows the location. She's been there. That kind of recon's too valuable."

"There are ways to buy the information, Mr. Ford," Pildi said, his voice soft. "All parts of the Congo basin are *in-hah-bee-ted*. I have contacts and organization. Indeed I do. Given the general vacinity, we can acquire commercial satellite photography. Given cash I can acquire private information. I can assure you, she is not critical."

So I popped it on him, and popped it on Abdul. "My bottom line isn't diamonds. I intend to have him arrested and tried. If she's been fronting for him and can provide details that nail a conviction, so much the better."

"Arrest whom? Moshid? In whose court would he be tried?"

"I'll figure that out. Right now I want her wired to us."

"But—"

"The tactical consideration, Major. We go shoot up a base camp then look for his diamonds? You know, you and your people could do that, do that right now without Abdul and me. I think she knows where he keeps his stash. I don't want to go treasure hunting in a jungle. I've had enough of that."

Pildi's teeth flashed, a shark with a belly laugh. "But that's pree-cise-lee what we *are* doing, treasure hunting in a jungle. Or robbing a thief in the jungle, to be accurate. You're right, I could do this myself, but I suspect a . . . a *wired* relationship with you could prove useful to me, in a longer term." He raised an eyebrow, tilting the bowler incongruously, amusing himself. Then he asked, "You are sure you've no other interests in her, Mr. Ford?"

"Aw, crap. Pildi, I—"

"But you speak to me of tactical considerations, Mr. Ford. Allow me to analyze your proposal. You are being much too complicated in your planning, sir. KISS. Kay-Eye-Ess-Ess. Keep It Simple, Stupid. This is the essence of military operations, at least the ones that work. No, no, before you argue, *listen* to me. I know who this Moshid is. He has supplied weapons for all sides, and yes, he has worked for Saddam. He used his contacts in Saddam's secret armament network to build his own arms organization. I suspect he has worked for your CIA as well, certainly he has contacts with the French. Perhaps he consorted with your Nicholson?"

"If Ted did that it was to get close to him."

"Earth is littered with good excuses for cohabiting with devils. Good God. Someone has protected Moshid, for whatever reasons. I believe you wish to destroy him. The way you stop a blood-drenched butcher is not through weakness. You kill him, you finish him. To attempt to capture him and then try him? If you find a court, if you *create* a court, who protects him will appear."

"I'd love that."

"You think so? I'd bet not," Pildi huffed.

"You'd lose that bet . . . Are you in, Major?"

He bit his lower lip, cast a cockeyed gaze at the elephant. "You do not listen to me well, I believe."

"Fifteen to twenty thousand carats. And nine antiaircraft missiles."

"American?"

"No, Russian."

"Not the best product, nor so reliable."

"I'm kicking in five hundred thousand dollars to get it started. Clean money. My own money. I'll transfer it to any account you specify."

"*Your* money? I cannot lose, eh? . . . Now answer me, Ford. Why trust me?"

"I know something about Africa. I can tell you and Mosoke aren't short term. You both see a future."

Pildi chuckled, a chuckle that rippled from his shoulders down to his knees. "What future lies beyond fifteen thousand carats?"

"You're no cynic."

His eyes narrowed, fractionally. "I've a dozen very good men, the *reliable* ones with whom *my* back is safe. . . . Let me begin to consider the details. I have some leeway in how to *structure* the operation?"

"Absolutely."

"How much risk are you willing to assume, personally?"

"I'll be out there with you."

"This is no safari, Mr. Ford."

"Commandos don't hunt diamonds, either, Major Pildi."

Now his eyes narrowed to slits. "A Silicon Valley investor in the African bush war—so interesting a combination."

"One that provides, say, a bandit leader, or a rogue guerrilla commander, you know, a stud who has a *knack* for tactical deception, with a couple of interesting gimmicks to exploit, doesn't it?"

He smiled, uneasily. Now he *knew* I didn't give a damn about the diamonds.

"Pildi . . . Are you in?"

"I must arrange details in Kampala."

"That's a yes? Lay it on the line."

"It's a yes."

Abdul peered around the back of the elephant. "She's returning. . . . She is. She's walking back along the lake. Neaves didn't go all the way around the track."

Raising one of his long fingers, with an odd gentleness, Pildi said, "At this point, I believe, as I see our plan and the culmination—what I'm saying is, we don't need her, Ford. . . . You, however, seem damned set on her."

"Here's my best outcome, Pildi. I want to convict Moshid in a court of law."

Pildi shook his head. "A war crimes tribunal is a fantasy of righteousness."

I didn't answer him. Elise was coming back, and she appeared to be looking around for me.

Pildi offered me his hand. I shook it.

"We'll talk again."

"Yes."

I slapped Abdul on the shoulder and he nodded.

I walked out of the garden toward the track, shouting, "Hey, Elise . . . Wait there."

When I met her at the track she was sweaty but not out of breath. She asked, "What's over there?" She pointed toward the trees, not the boat dock.

"A garden, bushes cut like exotic animals. Saw a syringe on the ground—heroin addicts shoot dope by the hippo."

"How's your ankle?"

Damn, is she smart, to try to trick me with a switch

like that. "You mean my heel? It still hurts, like a stone bruise. . . . Did I tell you I hurt my ankle?"

"I don't remember."

"You didn't run all the way around, huh?"

"No, I decided to come back for you. I wondered if you were really hurting."

I laughed. "Are you suspicious of me? For what? You're the goddamn spy, sticking me up for two hundred grand."

She shrugged.

I leaned forward, put my hands on my thighs, put my face in hers, nose to nose. "So, gorgeous, whyn't you tell me what you want to do with the money. Huh? I've been real straight about this. Let's cut the games. I get my damn ankle hurt and you're a cop."

"You said it was your heel."

"It is my heel."

"You just said ankle."

"I'm highly suggestible, Elise. You *screw* with my mind and I'll say anything. Here, want to see the damn lump on my foot?"

"I've no interest in your lumps, not at the moment." She had her tongue on the top of her lip. She turned her head, sharply, her ear brushing my nose, tweaking it, actually. I stood up straight, put my hand on my nose. She ignored it, looked over at the garden. "Is that supposed to be a giraffe?"

I could take that question where I needed to go, so I jumped it. "Giraffe, hippo, lion, crocodile, the complete menagerie, Elise. It's a European idiot's Africa, quaint animals, no people, no automatic weapons, no valuable minerals."

She rolled her eyes. "Don't be so stuffed with shit. It's a gardener cutting bushes for children."

"It's that," I said, "and the son of a bitch has an imagination. The guy's a clip artist, uses flowers in the brush. The snake has violet eyes. . . . Want to go look?"

"I prefer a hot tub," she said. She turned, started jogging again. As she hit her stride she said over her shoulder *"Au revoir."*

I SHOWERED. PILDI'S ACCUSATION BIT. A FANTASY OF self-righteousness. I've had those. Pildi saw the diamonds as ammo for his tribe and I'm talking United Nations war crimes. The man was right.

Elise wasn't in her room, nor was she in the restaurant. I ordered a salad. Okay, we could work this without her. Maybe I am trying to do too much, I thought.

MIDAFTERNOON, I WANDERED DOWNSTAIRS, WALKED out to the breezeway by the lake, walked over the flagstone path past the hotel swimming pool.

I heard a soft whistle. She surprised me, stretched out in a chaise longue, wearing a bikini and beetly sunglasses, a thumb stuck in the middle of a paperback.

My eyes ran from her face, over the sharp chin, her breasts stretching the gold nylon, down the rippling line of muscle on her abdomen, over her legs slick with sunscreen.

"How is your ankle, Peter?"

"My heel, Elise. I soaked it."

She started to look at her paperback, instead closed it

and flipped it onto the flagstones, a look of disgust on her face. "It's a book about money," she said.

"How to get it or lose it?"

"Reading it tires me. It reminds me that I'm waiting for money." She looked around on the ground. "I had a drink here."

"Left side, underneath."

Her hand flopped around underneath the chair.

"No, back—five centimeters."

Frustrated, she sat up, pulled up the sweating glass of faint brown stain in melting ice. "An afternoon scotch. And I don't like scotch. And I hate Switzerland." She took a sip, a slurp with her tongue, the sunglasses slipping slightly down her nose. "Waiting is a prison, Peter. . . . I spent seven years in an orphanage waiting for parents. A state orphanage. The fucking *glory* of France." Her lips hooked into a deep frown, a dark edge. With a flick of her wrist she kicked back the scotch and gulped it down, leaving nothing.

"You want another one?"

"No."

"I'll buy you a bottle."

"I don't want anything from you."

"Yeah you do." I went over and picked up her book, set it down right at the curve of her hip.

I started to walk off.

"Where are you going?" she asked.

"To soak my heel," I replied.

I HAD A GOOD THEORY, NOW, A GODDAMN CRACKLING theory. Seven years in an orphanage, and with her looks. They'd see, they'd think, they'd do it because they'd done it before. They'd take her and train her and prime her. The glory of France. That's no con, that's a tough woman leaking, her psyche leaking with afternoon scotch. Name your bet and I'll triple it. She'd been raised by French intelligence officers to be an operative. The French used orphans like that, and sometimes the kids knew each other, thought of each other as brothers and sisters. Raised to be an operative. What a joke, on her, on me.

I was beginning to buy into her. Somebody raised with a mission, a mission pounded into her, and she reaches a point where she realizes it's all grab ass and crap. Her greed was her sanity, her new mission. Maybe she had a point. Maybe she was ahead of me.

TWENTY MINUTES LATER I WAS IN MY ROOM, PUTting on a bathing suit, thinking about going down to the hot tub and sauna, or boiling myself in the steam room.

I heard a knock at the door, one steel thump.

Her hair was frizzy. She wore a rumpled white bathrobe over her bathing suit, leather sandals on her feet. I could smell the scotch on her breath.

Not even the French can teach an agent to make love like that.

You can't. It's impossible.

"YOU'RE ANGRY," SHE SAID. "AS ANGRY AS YOU WERE in the desert." Her head lay on the pillow. Her eyes were red, exhausted, no mellow to them.

I decided not to argue with her.

She came out with it. "Nicholson told me you're rich as sin and you hired an assassin to kill Moshid."

Was that the first time she'd said his name?

I turned my head toward her. "The first time I ever heard Moshid's name was last week, in Paris, when Guyton told me that same bullshit story about an assassin. . . . But he's the guy, the nurse killer? The jumpsuit who killed the nurse after Desert Storm? What's Moshid's deal, Elise? Who protects him? Guyton said the man's moved weapons in Congo and Angola. Who supplies Moshid? Was Nicholson setting him up, going to feed him weapons then try something? Or were they in business together?"

She didn't reply. She looked at her breasts, then rolled up on her elbow, put her finger in my hair.

So I told her.

You don't have this fact.

Burundi 1975. Right there in bed I walked her down the savage green path. I just told her the facts. I was fifteen, back from school in Massachusetts. The ambassador learned of the trouble at Kovalu Station. Dad was the ambassador's number two and when the word got to the embassy he knew and suddenly he was a mess and no one blamed him for being a mess. So Dr. Gunther and I left him at the embassy in Bujumbura, his red face drained to a color this side of dry ash. Gunther and I went alone in a *L'Hopital* Land Rover, the *L'Hopital* symbol easing us through roadblocks, allowing the Land Rover to glide through the chaos like a four-wheeled magic carpet. We drove the fifty klicks to Kovalu. The rebels—thieves, really— had dropped the bridge so we had to slop through the stinking culvert and walk the last five hundred meters. I took a machete out of the backseat and I gripped that machete as we walked down that black mud path,

knowing. The green walls of jungle didn't hide anything. I remember my sweat, the slick moisture on all
of it, the trees, the mud, my face, hot and humid
breath you choke on. I ran the last fifty meters to the
station, Gunther stumbling behind me. Blankets and
clothes lay scattered in front of the supply hut, torn
clothes, emptied clothes trunks gaping, bandages
from the infirmary spilling out of cardboard crates.
Mother's body, in her nurse's uniform, was discovered in the heap of bodies behind the infirmary out-
house. I didn't discover her, Gunther did. Dr. Gunther
had seen worse. Up to then I hadn't.

See, the soldiers guarding the station had fled, out of
fear, cowardice, corruption.

As he reached for a blanket to cover her body Gunther tried to talk. He muttered that I shouldn't see this—
but the old man wanted me to see it. The way she fell,
lying over those dead children, my mother died trying to
protect the goddamned innocent. Gunther saw that. Dr.
Gunther tried to say something, but nothing came out.
The old boy's lips didn't work. He dropped the blanket
over her. Then his hand balled up into a fist. He put his
fist on my shoulder and I'll swear his fist felt like the
dark weight of the earth.

Now you have that fact.

"I really despise soldiers," I said to Elise, "who don't
do their duty."

Her stare was intense, yet disarmed and utterly convinced.

Her eyes moved from me to the ceiling, to the thin
slat of afternoon light shining through the break in the
dark crimson window drapes.

A moment later she kissed me on the lips.

I WATCHED HER DRESS, THAT THIN SLAT OF LIGHT A slash on her body.

"Moshid killed that nurse? In Iraq?" she asked.

"Yes," I replied.

She started for the door, then paused.

"The diamonds they found on Nicholson's body, Peter. I believe . . . I think Nicholson got them from a man named Brune."

Now we're getting somewhere, I thought.

"Jimmy Duke Brune?"

"Is that his name?"

"He died in a plane crash in Sierra Leone, didn't he?"

"So I heard."

"Why would Brune give Nicholson twenty-five or thirty thousand dollars' worth of diamonds?"

She shrugged.

"Who told you that he got the diamonds from Brune?"

She waited, clearly thinking. "Nilo," she said.

She said it tired and sweet, and it sounded a lot like the truth.

I BUZZED HER ROOM ABOUT SEVEN BUT SHE DIDN'T answer the phone. Before I went downstairs to dinner I knocked on her door. Silence, dull silence. I called her name. No answer.

I ate a salad then went for a walk, a long one around the jogging track. As I walked my mind got onto hotel rooms where no one answers, my dad on the red carpet in that awful room in the Hotel Cronos, the oblivion in that room. By the time I reached the edge of the lake I forced myself to quit thinking about that history. The lake was still and utterly calm. The sun was almost down, a red gash along the edge of the mountains, a gray photo haze on the water's surface.

Back in the hotel I walked upstairs and I tapped on her door. Again, no answer. I went into my room, out to the balcony, like an idiot peered around the buttress at her balcony. Her balcony door was shut, the red curtains pulled tight. Though it left a dry taste in my mouth I'd told myself a story. See, it was a story, not a theory, because it was desire with no facts. The story said she'd gone out by herself, to walk by the lake to sort things out, to get her head untangled. That's what I'd told myself, as if her head were tangled.

I went down to the hotel bar and bought a bottle of whiskey. In my room I had one small drink, no ice, told myself she had to be untangling. I kicked off my shoes and fell asleep.

THE NEXT MORNING, BREAKFAST AND NO ELISE.

I knocked on her door and got no response. I was no longer puzzled, I wasn't telling myself a story, I was flat worried. I went in my room, phoned hers, and let it ring a dozen times. I could hear her phone ringing through the wall. No answer. So I called the maid service. I said Miss Neaves had left something in her room and we needed to get it.

The maid came up, opened the door to Elise's room. A half-empty bottle of scotch sat on the dresser. The bed wasn't slept in, her bag was gone.

The maid had a perfect, noncommittal stare.

"Help me find her mobile phone," I said. After looking under the bed and in the bathroom, I shrugged, grabbed the bottle of scotch, went out into the hallway.

Damn. I pulled out my key chain. Yeah, the Audi key
was still there. I ran my finger through the groove, found
a faint trace of green clay. She'd taken an impression.
When? The gift tie, man, when she brought me the tie. I
stuck the bottle of scotch in my room then headed for the
garage. The Audi was not where I'd parked it. I walked
through the garage—no black Audi. I returned to my
hotel room. Everything seemed checked out except . . .
Klix's phone, Moshid's code phone. *The code phone was
missing.* My throat constricted. What the hell? Now try
and figure that. I started walking fast, too fast, so I made
myself slow down. I went to the front desk. Did she
check out? No, the clerk replied, she's still registered,
her room on the account of Mr. Ford.

I walked across the lobby, going over it. Now, she's
taken the car and she planned the grab. It's a rental,
she's not listed as the driver, but she's wise. Odds are
good she'll beat any kind of border control, so few
check anything anymore. They'll see her European
passport and she'll pass through. Would she head for
Prague? Moshid wouldn't be in Rome. And Samir—
well, I doubted he was still alive. That was something
Nicholson hadn't counted on when he spread his story
that I had bought a hit man to take down Moshid, that
one of Saddam's chief financial operatives would get
snared. Murder by coincidence. No, not coincidence,
murder by proximity. Spies out there banging into one
another and Moshid a well-trained sociopath who understood someone unbuyable wanted to nail him. He
and Samir knew each other, didn't they? What had he
told Samir to get him to come to Rome? I'd had Samir
right from the start. He was in the life. As for Elise—I
thought I had her right. She didn't copy the key yester-

day, though, did she? And Moshid's phone. Could she
juice it? How would she use it without a current code?
What use, other than signals analysis to trace calls on
the phone via commercial communications channels?
Too damned sophisticated. Where would she buy that
capability? Or did the bitch have a code key . . .

I walked into the breezeway, plopped down at a
table. The seat didn't feel right. When the waiter came I
ordered a capuccino. The seat pained my back and butt.
No, I'd bet Elise wasn't running to Moshid.

After the capuccino put some caffeine snap in my
brain I went back to the garage, questioned the garage
manager. He had no record of the Audi leaving. Hotel
guests come and go as they please. You merely flash the
ticket stub, monsieur. My Bulgarians at the entrance
smile when you flash the proper ticket.

As I walked across the broad front lawn toward the
jogging track I ran through four or five more possibilities. That was it, mental exercise. Let's do something
positive with this and go with what you've got. Make the
right arrangements and Elise has ditched herself. If she
was on her way to Moshid what could she tell him? That
Nicholson owed Ford several hundred thousand bucks?

If she was on her way to Moshid I'd take the bet it
wasn't to sell me out.

I started around the park track, reached the two kilometer mark, walked from there to the animal garden. It
was a hunch and a bad hunch that came to nothing. The
parking lot on the far side of the garden was empty, except for a man with a broom sweeping litter into a gray
plastic sack. See the failed theory? She hadn't left but
was observing me? Toss that concept into the trash.

In the garden I wandered through the lion and hippo

shapes, bright flowers in the bush beasts, and noticed a dirty plastic syringe lying on the ground below the elephant's rump.   •

MY ASSUMPTIONS—IF I'D KNOWN ABOUT ELISE AND Dominique, if I'd had any inkling beyond that code phone. Perhaps I should have told Elise I knew about Dominique, that I knew who she was, what she did in Aruba, even asked sarcastically how a pro like Dominique had screwed up so big time in the *Peace Warrior* incident. What would Elise have said? Would she have told me why Dominique was rattled that night in Aruba, after she explained to Dominique who I was, told Dominique how she met me in the desert, told Dominique what I saw, told me how Dominique reacted oddly, lost her detachment, began to press her for more details, to ask her about this Ford, and Nicholson—yes, Dominique knew of Nicholson—to get the details of what I saw, to demand pictures, those pictures taken by the Americans at the river, of Jumpsuit and his victims. Would that knowledge have changed, substantially, what I arranged? What if I had known Dominique's angle? But I didn't know, I had glimpses of assassins, fragments of conversations gleaned from being on the periphery, on the edges, I had silhouettes, forms, contours. Yes, I've married some bad guesses. I've never argued that I'm totally rational. I've been honest with you, just like I was honest with the shrink. If I'd known Dominique's game I'd have gone out there anyway. The propellant of my own obsession with a fantasy of justice, an obsession fueled by shameful memories of Abdul's village torched by an army we'd just crushed, the pro's embarrassment at murder in my gunsights, that peroxide taste that won't dissipate, the stupid but to-the-bone guilt of Gunther's heavy fist laid on my frightened teenage shoulder, my money, the technology and people it buys, Pildi's convenient organization, the ability to strike. Damn. *I couldn't see anything else.*

As I stood there in the garden I couldn't see anything else.

I left the garden zoo, headed back to the track and the lake. At the boardwalk I stopped and watched the tourist steamer chugging out, not too much of a crowd on board. The boat had one of those cabins that jammed up close to the bow, a half-dozen kids on the stern, waving. The engines drove with a quiet thrum, the screws kicking up a low wash, the boat wake a slow turbulence on the flat, still surface.

IN THE HOTEL LOBBY I PULLED OUT MY MOBILE phone and punched in Abdul's number. No answer. The computer-generated German voice said I could leave a message. I didn't. Abdul had taken Pildi back to Zurich. I could rent another car and try to link up with him there or just wait and we'd get my money on Monday. Then we'd both go to Uganda and do it Pildi's way. Or maybe—could I expect that bank to be open? If the guy had gone ahead and transferred the funds we could get that moving right now.

I went to the bank and it was open. The teller checked the account—eight hundred grand on deposit since Friday morning. I left instructions for the bank officer, gave him the phone number of a hotel in Kampala, Uganda.

I tried Abdul again, this time I left a message. I told him to pick me up at the *hauptbahnhof.* I didn't know which train, but I'd grab the next express. He was to call me ASAP, assuming the phone would work on board the train. If we didn't connect, meet the next express.

As I checked out of the hotel I left a letter for Elise at the front desk, just in case. I told her she could reach me through Guyton in Paris.

The express train to Zurich left one minute late.

In Zurich Abdul met me in the train station. He had a different rental car, a good attitude and a decent argument.

"You do understand, sir, Pildi has had no time to prepare *anything,*" Abdul said as we walked through the train station. "I put him on the plane to Kampala last night."

"What concerns you, Abdul? Be specific."

He said, sounding textbook, "Operations should never be rushed and haphazard."

"You learn that in CIA spy school?"

His jaw thrust forward. "Don't talk down to me, please."

"I'm not. And if I am, I'm sorry, I'm talking to you like my father talked to me. You know how that happens. Let me show you something. Think through this dynamically, pieces and personalities in motion. Pildi's organized, Abdul, Pildi lives in a politically complex world, and he's organized, for shifts in personal loyalties, tribal allegiances, new opportunities. The elements fit, instantly. All we need is directed energy, audacity, Abdul, no sitting on our collective butts. You heard him, the man's talking commercial satellite imagery. He's what I sized him up to be—he's able and capable. Now, think motive, Abdul. You, me, we've our reasons to take down Moshid and his organization. Pildi's isn't simply diamonds or weapons. He has long-term goals. I've met men like him. They either end up dead or heads of state. For a man who thinks forward, like he does, Moshid's diamonds are chump change. He'll be most reliable, at least for this operation. We're going through with it."

"But she left you, with no word! *You* consider motive, Pete. She's a criminal, a *French* criminal—and you aren't worried?"

"Yeah, I'm worried. Frankly, I don't think she's a criminal. She's not a criminal, that's cover, and ineffective cover. She's still a French agent."

"Agent or criminal, we're potentially compromised, and we still go through with it? Because you've invested five hundred grand?"

Based on his eye-popping reaction, my glance must have been acid and withering. Better that glance than an angry jab. Me, wanting to strike him, punch Abdul for God's sake. Hell, he was already so bruised. You know I had to be angry—and of all people, of all people to get pissed at. I didn't have to spill to this kid about his village. He lived it, survived it, while we watched his parents and that nurse get slaughtered.

When his eyes retracted, and we stepped into the street, heading for his car, Abdul muttered, "I didn't mean it like it sounded, sir." Then he added, with a shrug. "Okay . . . Audacity." And he let it go at that.

CHAPTER 14

My Raid, Her Revenge

FROM THE HELICOPTER THE CHINKO RIVER WAS LESS the proverbial tortured brown snake and more an insane scrawl of water, a baffling chug of ginger ink, mad loops with the hung commas and accents of oxbow lakes rambling over a chunky green blanket of dense, dark jungle.

The chopper dipped lower, into a low-viz, terrain-hugging flight profile. We were well beneath the clouds, the denizens of the rainy season's five soaking months, but it was early morning and the clouds—not yet massed for deluge—lumbered about like nimbus galleons in a sea of bright sunlight.

I pulled my sunglasses out of the case in my camouflage uniform, looked back down at the river.

The Haut Chinko in the Central African Republic certainly wasn't my beat, nor had it been my father's. Though one time I'd been in Haut-Zaire province of the

Congo, in fact, just south of the border where the Chinko meets the Bomu branch of the Oubangui, I'd never set foot in the Central African Republic. That would change pronto as combat boots met Chinko mud.

The Central African Republic gets reduced to an acronym, the CAR, one that diplomats actually use. The CAR's isolation and anarchy made it a perfect spot for Moshid to retreat. Acquire an airfield and the Chinko region's centrality to Africa's various battlefields made it not so much an ideal weapons and supply laager, but a convenient spot to monitor various business transactions, to trade diamonds for bullets, a base from which to send a strike team to enforce a broken contract, a highly defensible nowhere to retreat to and fade when enforcement failed and discretion prevailed.

As for the big question, which Elise had not answered: who had let Moshid set up shop? The Central African Republic was still essentially a French protectorate, though French influence really didn't extend past the suburbs of the capital, Bangui, or the uranium works at Bakona. And here, in the southeast, the only outsiders were poachers after the elephants and giraffes that had been driven off the savannahs into the thick vegetation, or the unusual oil or mineral company with the balls to send geologists into the mud, murk, and tsetse flies.

No, Elise hadn't bothered to answer. Who had let Moshid set up shop along the Chinko? I had facts and hints, but nothing definite. Pildi's purchased data, the routes of ingress and egress, the locations, the photos he'd acquired of Moshid's cleverly disguised airfield, those items of information were top notch. But who permitted Moshid? That was the way to put it, who allowed the man to operate? That was opaque and hazy. Shine a bright light on it and all you got were gray shapes and photon scatter.

I'd thought about it. Based on what I knew I really had only four or five candidates, but because of my own determination to act, to get my ass *out* there, I'd decided that rather than theorize I'd see what or who emerged. I would also learn a lot based on who replaced Moshid after he was gone. In the back of my mind that was a goal, to stick around and see who took over his weapons operation.

I know operating without knowing who's who runs great risks. Abdul was right to urge caution. Operations can be rushed but by damn if you're pressing the accelerator you'd better know the other drivers and the road. However, at that precise moment in time I had the instrument to act, the means to compensate for what you know I saw as my failure at the river. You've got *all* those miserable facts, the lot of them. Now, for all I know you're a goddamn sophisticate and you have the ability to cool your passions and compartmentalize all your faults and blame everyone else for your indecisiveness, your lies, your cruelties, your brutalities. Such a perfect consumer you are, such a perfect, perpetual audience, fit to judge, gossip, sit on your ass and watch. But you—how will you react if you ever get the instrument? What happens to you if suddenly all of the pieces fall into place and you have the *power* to act and correct? You must understand what a trip that is. I had it all, money, crack troops, the ability to acquire what looked like reliable information, an instant logistics network in a corner of the planet I had the arrogance to presume I understood. That was all there. In retrospect I admit I wasn't completely rational, my money and my motives allowed me to weld fantastic speculation to complex facts, and money and motives and military confidence are powerful drugs, absolutely psychotropic, more powerful than the wonder drug of Wall Street capitalism, because motive breeds righteousness and military prowess breeds crusade. Listen to the language I use to describe it — it's on the edge or out into a purple orbit of the absurd, but that was the pulse I felt, that was the adrenaline, the same damn pump of the race through the desert to the river. And Lord forgive me, that's what I wanted, to recover that moment again, before the fact of the atrocity. I mean, my language at least gives you the drunken stagger of the delusion. I was *living* it — guns, money, self-righteousness, the glory of my own cleverness. In retrospect I was stupid and irrational, but my stupidity and irrationality were so effectively submerged in the arcana of running my own personal war machine that you have to believe I had no idea what a super con job I was laying on myself.

ON THE HELICOPTER: MY GAZE SHIFTED FROM THE brown river below me to the latest satellite imagery, the photos in the folder on my lap. See, my delusion was supported by such hard facts. The satellite photos were commercial imagery, now a week old, but with a resolution of a half meter. I mean, I could see his garbage pit from space, for God's sake.

We saw more than that, actually. Pildi had a pal who ran an Internet café in Kampala (the man had a master's in computer science from Georgia Tech) do a zoom and enhancement job on the sat photos. You still had to know how to interpret the images to understand what you were looking at, and to appreciate the technical expertise of Moshid's camouflage. Ultimately the shadows and edges, the not quite natural play of darkness and light, gave the site away as something other than a depression in the jungle not far from a long abandoned leprosarium.

I put a small magnifying glass to the top print. Moshid must have consulted his Iraqi and Serb friends on how to spoof satellites and air recon, though admittedly an airfield's hard to hide, even one carefully clipped from the jungle and shrouded with camouflage nets laced by natural vine, the landing strip further cloaked by potted trees and clumps of brush mounted on mobile trellises of chicken wire. In the floating expansion of the magnifying glass the trees looked great, until you picked out the oblong shadow and realized that was the darkness cast by a not-quite-hidden airplane wing, probably a twin-engine piston aircraft of some sort. How often did weapons supply planes use the airfield? Perhaps they didn't. My money had opened mouths. "I talked to people who have dealt with him," Pildi had said in Kampala when he told me how he had located Moshid's base. He rubbed his fingers together, gleefully. "There are few secrets." Pildi had made inquiries in Mbuji Mayi and Kisangani. Moshid preferred to ship directly from Ukraine, Serbia, and Cyprus, or swing the deal from Shanghai and Singapore. As of twelve hours ago another contact in Mbuji Mayi had assured Pildi by satellite phone that Moshid was still "up the Chinko." "This source," Pildi had said, with awe, "she is certain he is there. She's a man friend there, a mechanic on his plane. Money means no secrets, Peter."

No, I didn't read the intensity in Pildi's voice as the energy of his own delusion.

I slipped the satellite airfield photo into the folder behind my new corporate letterhead. Pildi knew how to spend money and knew how to keep operational security. At the moment we were partners in a Ugandan-based oil exploration venture. Loflin-Akama Exploration, and I was Mr. Loflin. That was the cover for the helicopter with extended-range fuel tanks and for the purchase of satellite imagery. The venture cover had cost me another five hundred grand. Unfortunately, we also had a partner, one that I would meet. Right after he cackled over money's power to open mouths, Pildi swore that our operation wouldn't be compromised. I knew very little about the partner other than he had to come to make certain that fifteen to twenty thousand carats worth of diamonds didn't destroy a carefully managed international market. Pildi said the partner's presence was excellent insurance. I argued with Pildi. No, Pildi said, this is insurance, the best insurance. The conglomerate is concerned that someone would have hoarded so many quality carats. They don't give a rat's ass about anything but money, I said. Precisely, Pildi said. If anything they would believe hoarded diamonds are a threat to their market sta-bill-it-tee.

Because I was stupid and irrational and dead set on getting out there I decided to roll with it—lingo for going along with something I knew was infinitely compromising.

THE HELICOPTER BANKED AS I LOOKED AT ANOTHER print in the folder. Pildi knew a big game hunter who ran contract safaris out of Bangui. Pildi had told him that one of the oil venture investors had asked about hunting in the area. Pildi had said the hunter had snickered, but, on the promise that Pildi would send him the sucker's business, came up with a trail map, such as it was. The map was computer-generated, with ground positioning satellite (GPS) markings. The last tick mark the hunter had on the map was still some fifty-five kilometers from Moshid's airfield. I'd labeled that Point One, and it was where the helicopter would land. The hunter didn't even have a mark on the old leprosarium. The hunter had written a note, by hand, in green ballpoint ink: "I know of no one who has been by watercraft down the Chinko, Songopai to Rafai. I know of no one who has visited the site of the old leper colony. According to a former French official in Bangui, the leper colony was abandoned in 1928 when plague killed most of the lepers and all but four of the medical staff. There was an airfield at the colony, apparently now lost to jungle. As far as I am aware, no one has been in there since. I do not believe the ivory poachers go that far. They've no helicopters and as you can see from the map there are no roads. Two herpetologists did visit Songopai two years ago and went down river (twenty kilometers??? not far) to collect black mambas. They collected snakes and returned via an ELF-Aquitaine helicopter. The region is really under no one's control. This makes organizing a hunt a problem. Unfortunately, safaris must be concerned about kidnapping. However, if your investor is interested, I am interested."

Pildi had paid the hunter five hundred bucks for the map and his research. He'd attached a receipt.

I looked at the enhanced sat photo, the magnified

remnants of the leprosarium. Like a thick disease the jungle had eaten the place, swallowed it and absorbed it. Only the vaguest shape of one deteriorated structure remained, the central hospital. Ah, but the shadows under the foliage. Beneath the decay were nine cylindrical huts, possibly inflatables. You'd have to guess they were for weapons storage.

THE HELICOPTER SWEPT CLOSER TO THE RIVER, THE downdraft from its blades adding white chop to the brown surface. The pilots said they were British contractors out of Kenya and I acted like I believed them. They returned the favor by pretending I was an oil company executive, grinning coolly when they saw my camouflage fatigues. In the small talk before the flight they'd mentioned they'd flown for Pildi before, and rarely on missions with flight plans. They'd flown Pildi and his men out two days earlier, a long flight from the town of Faradje in the Congo. Our flight plan called for taking photos from the air of the Garamba National Park in Congo and to land in Bondo, another Congo town. Of course the deviation in the CAR, a deviation of two hundred kilometers, was never mentioned.

"Right below us, Mr. Loflin," the pilot said. "Your party."

I heard him through the headphones and said, "I see the rafts."

"Are you certain, sir, you want to stay out here for *five* days?"

"I told you," I said, trying to sound irritated, "I like to hunt. We're going to scout this out for a safari."

THE WRONG SIDE OF BRIGHTNESS   199

The pilot replied with a grin and a stiff nod. "Call us when you need us," the copilot said.

THE HELICOPTER DEPARTED.

Pildi walked out from the tree line to greet me, so tall and Dinka in his green jungle camouflage uniform with slash streaks of brown. A dark blue beret rode his head like a jaunty sneer cocked to the right.

After shaking hands with Pildi I met our other investor. He was a Brit, decked out in jungle camouflage and a carny smile on a pudgy face that I could see even through the insect netting that dropped from the brim of his hat to his neck. The man had an odd waddle in his walk. He reeked of one hundred percent DEET insect repellent.

"Martel," he said, offering his hand. "And you are *Loflin.*"

I shook his hand. Our eyes locked and he knew I couldn't stand him.

PILDI, TWO OF HIS MEN, AHTEE AND A MAN WHO

went by Tango, put my gear in the assault raft.

After he'd stashed my gear Tango handed me a silenced MP-5 submachine gun. "Here, Loflin," he said. "Here . . . You can use, eh? Major Pildi says you use." Tango had an endless grin of yellow teeth, one lower tooth covered with a stainless steel cap.

I noticed Martel and Ahtee, staring at one another. Martel was tough to read, Ahtee wasn't. The Dinka grimaced and shook his head. When Ahtee saw me, he pursed his lips.

THE RAFT WAS REALLY AN UPGRADED LIGHT RECON Boat, brown-colored, with a small gas-powered motor. The assault boat was big enough for ten men. There would be five of us, initially.

Now all of us put on boonie hats fitted with insect netting, even the Dinkas. We pulled the netted insect scarves down over our faces. We put on gloves, shoved out into the river, using our hard plastic paddles to keep us near the bank, to avoid any stray aircraft. The Chinko's strong current, about five to six kilometers an hour, would carry us to Point Two, a position slightly less than forty kilometers from Moshid's airfield. The petrol engine was for an emergency return upriver, if that proved to be necessary.

I stationed myself behind Martel. Ahtee sat in the bow, Tango manned the stern, Pildi sat to my right.

THOSE FIRST TWO HOURS ON THE RIVER NO ONE spoke, the current propelled us, the cloud masses above us building and darkening, the humidity hell, the countless insects mad, noxious darts clinging to the netting, swarming over the surface and landing on the gunnels of the raft.

We passed a series of mud slicks on the near bank, like smooth belly slides into the river.

Martel swatted at a buzzing clutch of flies, glanced at me.

A moment later Martel turned his head, offered his carny smile, and said over his shoulder, "The crocs don't eat their prey in the water."

I ignored him.

"I say, the crock-o-diles don't eat their prey in the water."

I glanced at Pildi. I couldn't really see Pildi's face through the face netting and the boonie hat riding low on his forehead, but I could tell he wanted me to respond.

"I've lived in Kampala," I said.

"Oh? Know the lakes?" Martel replied. "So you know the crocs and their methods."

Crap, I thought, smart talk. Crocs and their methods. It was too hot and nasty for smart talk.

But Martel surprised me and canned it. Maybe he had been around.

ABOUT A QUARTER TO THREE IN THE AFTERNOON WE reached Point Two. Pildi's other men saw us coming. We pulled in, unloaded, and hid the boat.

Pildi's advance group consisted of fourteen men, giving us nineteen in all, counting Martel. Five were at Point Two, the other nine were ten kilometers up the trail, moving quietly, using machetes only as necessary. Those poor bastards were also lugging the light mortar, two light machine guns, and several kilos of plastic explosive.

"I take it we strike off immediately?" Martel asked Pildi.

Pildi said yes.

Martel surprised me again. I figured him for complaints, but there were none. Without another word he put on his "kit," a light aluminum frame and rucksack favored by special operations troops. He checked himself, checked the balance, all very pro.

Ahtee swung a small Carl Gustav recoilless rifle over his back. He pointed to a bandoleer with four of the eighty-four millimeter rounds. "You carry?" he asked me. I nodded, picked up the heavy ammunition, each round like a liter bottle of lead.

We went into the jungle. We walked, and no one said much of anything, even when we went through the swarm of African killer bees. Despite the face netting and fatigues I got hit on the neck, felt the burn, the nausea. I popped a Benadryl.

"Nasty, aren't they?" Martel intoned. "I'd rather face crocs."

"No you wouldn't," Tango said.

Tango had the netting over his face but I could tell he wasn't grinning.

SINCE THE ADVANCE PARTY HAD SCOUTED OUT A route—and they had the mortar—our group made about three klicks an hour, outstanding time for hard jungle. And Martel surprised me again. Despite the pudgy face and waddle he was in excellent shape.

But he muttered, occasionally glanced back at me, once or twice glanced at Tango and muttered some more.

We paused to take a water break. The tsetse flies swarmed. Martel pushed them away from his face, raised the netting, took a sip from his canteen. As he capped the canteen he muttered, "Fucking crocs you can dispatch with a rifle bullet."

"If you see the crocodile," Tango said.

Martel capped the canteen, slapping the top with the palm of his hand.

As I took a piss I watched Martel examine a branch on a tree. Out came his bowie knife. With a deft whack he cut the branch, started making himself a walking stick.

We moved out, Martel testing, then satisfied with his cane.

Maybe a half hour later, as we moved through a particularly thick ravine, Tango whispered to me, almost gleefully, "I haf irritated Martel."

"Where's he from?" I asked.

Tango shrugged.

"Have you seen him before?"

"Yes, in Kisangani with Major Pildi. Eight months ago. He flew in. Flew in on a small jet."

"Was he there to trade diamonds?"

"Major Pildi said he told our generals that however the war in Congo went, he wanted them to know he was cooperative."

I could believe that. In the deep gloom of the jungle ravine I checked my watch. It was seven P.M. We had made good time. Well, it hadn't rained, which was odd. I started walking faster, passing Martel and two other men, until I caught Pildi. Pildi had to be psychic. He had his radio out. "When we clear the edge of the ravine," he told me. "That should be GPS Point Three." It took ten minutes to climb out. Evening sunlight filtered through the canopy of trees and vines. Pildi broke squelch three times. Five seconds later our answer, the sound of squelch breaking four times in the static. A signal from Point Four. "We are within two kilometers of the forward team," Pildi said, as much to himself as to me.

THE CAMP WAS DAMNED PLEASANT, GIVEN THE CIR-
cumstances. They had a stove under a small ledge, with
wide brush fronds tied to stakes to deflect any heat signature from the smokeless fuel tablets. One of the two
men at the stove raised the pot and said "Gombo." Okra,
they were cooking.

Pildi sent three men forward to contact the sentinels.

Six of us in the second team, including Martel, sat
down, drank water, got *matoke* (plantains and stewed
beef) on a paper plate. Ahtee came up with a bottle of
pili pili sauce, a mix of onion, tomatoes, cayenne, and
who knows what else.

"Pil-dee, *pili pili,*" one of the men said. The other
Dinka laughed. Pildi had his insect netting rolled up
onto his boonie hat. Despite the rapid darkness about us,
his angular, rawboned face seemed to shine.

"Pil-dee, *pili pili,*" they said.

"An old joke," Pildi said to me with a stiff sigh.

"DAMN BAD PLACE FOR SNAKES," MARTEL SAID TO
me as we rigged our hammocks between two trees.
"Mambas. Do you know mambas, Mr. Loflin? They're
aggressive bitches. Cayenne's supposed to deter them
but it doesn't."

Martel knew what to do with that hammock. When
he'd finished with the hammock he slung his rucksack
on a line, staked the line, tossed the line over a limb and
raised his gear off the ground. He also checked his automatic pistol and bowie knife, then went about ten meters away from the hammocks to pee.

"Shit," he whispered, harshly.

I heard a thrashing in the darkness.

I sprang up with my submachine gun.

He emerged. It was too dark to see his face.

"What happened?" I asked.

"Snake of some sort," he said with disgust. "Not a mamba. They don't die that easily. . . . Do you have insect repellent handy?"

I tossed him a tube of my best stuff.

As he rubbed himself with the repellent, Martel said, "Major Pildi informs me you are concerned about my presence. Don't be, Mr. Loflin. I've an idea where we are but I definitely don't know where we are going. That isn't usually the way I operate. But, when Pildi approached my employer and said he would be encountering fifteen to twenty thousand carats worth of diamonds, with which my employer would love to have participation, my employer said I simply had to come along. That's a trove large enough to create a price fluctuation, should it end up in abusive hands. . . . Here's your insect repellent."

"Keep it," I replied.

AT THREE A.M. THE ADVANCE TEAM OF FIVE LEFT. AT four A.M. the remaining fourteen of us followed. I took my turn, carrying the mortar's base plate, taking the awkward metal bitch from Roger, Pildi's senior mortarman. There was no relief from the insects. Instead of flies there were swarms of hungry mosquitoes. Sunrise in the jungle, slow-motion mists rising amid the fast sound of birdcalls, birdcalls shrill and sharp surrounding you unseen—the effect would be eerie if all you had to do was watch and listen and enjoy the wonder. But move through raw jungle, live in it, feel the sweat

of each step, the fatigue of survival—there is no eeri-
ness.

We reached a break in the thick jungle, moved carefully out of the tree line. For a kilometer or so we
walked through tall saw grass, the blades rising to four
meters off the moist ground. There were a series of gaps
in the walls of grass. "Elephant," Ahtee said. A few minutes later he said, "Spoor." Yeah, huge mounds covered
with green flies. I didn't want to run into elephants.

"Poachers would do best to carry the ivory back to
the river, wouldn't they?" Martel said, to no one in particular. He poked the saw grass with his walking stick,
then ambled on.

Around seven-thirty we hit our GPS Point Five—by
the crow nineteen kilometers from Moshid's base.

By nine o'clock the heavy, humid air had settled on
us like a choking cloak. The thickness of it almost made
me yearn for the dust of the desert.

The rain hit us at a quarter to three in the afternoon.
For twenty minutes it was an impenetrable torrent,
crashing walls of water, and we literally clung to the
tree trunks. Then the heavy rain ended, became a drizzle, and we started moving, slipping through the muck.

I grazed my cheek, had to dope it with antibiotic. I
could feel the stubble of tsetse bites on my skin.

EARLY THAT EVENING WE HIT POINT EIGHT, FOUR
kilometers from the airfield. We dropped our gear,
formed a perimeter. I set up a satellite phone, turned on
the scrambler, got the sat phone linked to a satellite. I
punched in the number and Abdul answered. Since we'd
last talked he'd done the best he could. He was now

posing as a man with connections to a group that had acquired several thousand ex-Soviet assault rifles, which wasn't all that much of a pose. Abdul said the source in Mbuji Mayi believed Moshid was still at his base. However, the source said Moshid was expecting a delivery or something. Abdul had no details. An arms delivery? To the Chinko base? Abdul didn't know. He said he was passing on information he'd acquired for a hundred bucks and a bottle of Kentucky sour mash.

For dinner we ate MREs, then sacked out, guard duty pulled in hour-long shifts.

Pildi woke me at two A.M. He sent the lead element forward, Tango and four men wearing light-amplifying night vision goggles.

The rest of us followed an hour later. At four A.M. we rendezvoused at Point Nine, a spot near a trail crossing three hundred meters from a small clearing near the old leprosarium.

Tango, a dead cigar stuck in his mouth, his night vision goggles dropped around his neck, gave his recon report. First, they'd found a superb mortar position about one hundred fifty meters south, on a small rise. They'd put luminescent tape on the game trail that led to the position. Ahtee would take the mortar section there. As for the base area itself, as we suspected, Moshid had both low-tech and high-tech sentinels. Four guard dogs were on lines strung near the weapons huts. Our recon had identified two guards (both apparently asleep) in an observation bunker near what looked like the entrance to a larger bunker. There were also seismic monitors up the trail, just before you reached a three-meter-high fence strung with concertina razor wire and garlands of empty beer and coke cans.

"You didn't trigger the seismic alarms?"

"I walk on cotton," Tango replied confidently. "But, you listen? You hear electric generators? Loud. They shake the ground. Good cover for us."

"This fence didn't show up on the photos."

"It grows with bush," Tango said. "Good cover for us."

"We have to get through the fence and silence the dogs," I said.

"They're big dogs but they sleep, sleep even with the generators," Tango said, momentarily taking the unlit cigar out of his mouth. "The fence . . ." His yellow and steel teeth briefly clenched as he considered his options. "Best if we blow it, go quick," he nodded. "We bring four satchel charges, plastic explosive. We'll need two." He nodded again, the nod of a man who'd done it.

AHTEE TOOK ROGER AND ROGER'S ASSISTANT MOR-tarman to the mortar position. That left fifteen of us for the assault, plus Martel. Pildi intended to use four men as a base of fire, armed with a light machine gun and a heavy fifty caliber sniper rifle. There'd be an opening mortar barrage—Ahtee would drop the first mortar round when Pildi gave the order via radio. Simultane-ously, the machine guns and snipers would smash the guard post and take out the dogs. A satchel charge of plastic explosive, handled by me and Tango, would blow the fence. As the assault team went in, the mortar fire on the compound would lift. The rest should finish quickly.

THOSE FIRST GRAY MOMENTS OF DAWN BEGAN TO crack the jungle canopy.

Pildi turned to Martel, said stonily, "I told you to go with Ahtee."

"Well, you know Ahtee and I don't see quite eye to eye."

"From Kisangani? That isn't to matter."

Martel slouched, very so-what. He took his hat off. As he fiddled with the netting he said, "You know, Major, I haven't asked you about that mortar. What do you plan on hitting with it?"

"We didn't know how many men he might have," I said. "A mortar gives us an edge."

"Moshid keeps twenty men or so," Martel said, smoothly. "Most of them sleep down in the bunker, because it's air-conditioned. They're stupid thugs, Loflin, not professional soldiers like you and Pildi. Moshid has two bodyguards that could be trouble but here they spend most of their free time drinking and screwing. . . . They've five or six girls here. He gets them from the Sudan. Buys them from a friend in Khartoum."

Pildi and I looked at one another.

"Oh, yes, I've been here, gentlemen. I've dealt with Moshid, that's the business." Martel plumped his hat, dropped it back on his head. "Don't look so down, my friends. Moshid has cut a large swath in Africa, and made lots and lots of enemies." He shrugged. "This business, even the best of us make a few enemies. I was supposed to find out why you were his enemies, and determine if we can do business with you." He flashed his carnival grin. "Are you sure you haven't done a little time as a mercenary here in Africa, Mr. Loflin? I've met only one other oil executive with your expert field skills. Former Green Beret, he claimed. As for your men, Pildi, we can guarantee you and your people lucrative security contracts virtually any—"

Suddenly Pildi reached for Martel's throat, catching it and squeezing, getting throat, words, and a handful of insect net, slamming him against the trunk of a tree. "You've sold us *out,*" Pildi hissed.

Martel gasped, lost his walking stick, his hands grappling at Pildi's forearm. "Let go," Martel wheezed. "Shit, Moshid has no idea you're here. I can promise."

"You *lied,*" Pildi said. "Tricked *me.*"

Pildi had Martel off the ground, feet dangling, head wedged into the tree. Martel's face cherried.

"Don't kill him before he talks," I said. Damn, I was angry.

Martel, grasping Pildi's arm with his hand, whispered harshly, "You need political support for your people's guerrillas, we'll insure it. Dammit Major—it's in the *business.*"

Pildi stared at Martel—then dropped him.

Martel, again surprising me, landed with agility.

After gauging Pildi—and glancing at me—Martel bent forward, picked up his walking stick. "You two . . . the both of you need to understand," he wheezed. "It's . . . it's the nature of the business. Knowledge is the only fucking law, knowing whom you deal with and when to deal." He touched his throat, his head shaking from side to side. "Damn, you're a strong bastard, Pildi." Now Martel, with odd meticulousness, adjusted his face net. "Gosh." He swallowed again, fought another surge of trauma in his neck. "Well . . . I'll call you when I need someone choked." He coughed, then, his voice cracking, continued. "In my opinion, Moshid's as good as gone, for several reasons, not the least of them being you hard boys will march right through them. I can see you gentlemen know this business, but speaking as one professional to another, don't bother mortaring the pasture, just use grenades on the bunker, fire that recoilless rifle into the bunker entrance, follow up with grenades, tear gas if you have it. They'll pour out and then you finish it. Moshid keeps his diamonds in a safe in the back of the bunker. Which is another reason, to be truthful. See, we had Moshid figured for two thousand carats, at the most, sizeable but not a hoard. Twenty thousand? He's on his way to becoming a market problem."

"How did he get twenty thousand carats?" I asked.

Martel stared at me. "Sierra Leone," he said with a cool snap. Then he added, as if catching himself, "Now, that's an educated guess, Mr. Loflin. In Sierra Leone, Moshid—well, that all became such an embarrassing ruckus over there, didn't it? Too much news coverage and, well, too many disorganized opportunities for greedy people." He paused again. "Oh yes. There's a possibility Moshid might have a few lugs sleeping in one of the Quonsets, but they'll be stupid and drunk. I suppose you can kill them, too, if you want. . . . I'll go find Ahtee with his mortar—and stay out of your way." He ambled off toward the trail.

Pildi swung toward me, said in an angry, harsh whisper, "What? Do we do it?"

"We're set, so let's go," I hissed.

"Did you *imagine?*"

"Martel? No. But he's bought."

"Are you sure?"

"No. But we're here and if he's lying he's dead."

"Could we use grenades?"

"On the bunker? Fuck that, I want Moshid alive in front of a judge."

"What of Martel, Peter? He won't understand you."

"I'm going to follow him, make sure he links up with Ahtee."

"If he doesn't, *kill* him, *now*," Pildi said.

I followed Martel.

MARTEL MUST HAVE LISTENED. HE WAITED, THERE IN the darkness mottled by gray.

"I've my pistol," he whispered, calmly.

"I'm escorting you to the mortar position."

"If you think it's necessary, Loflin, have at it. I heard you two discuss killing me. That would be fatal to any long-term business associations. Think about it, Loflin. If I wanted to give you away, if *we* had wanted to give Pildi away, we'd have done it a week ago."

"Nature of the business?"

He didn't like my sarcasm. Even in the darkness I could see his head jerk. I could also see the pistol, gripped in his right hand. "Yes," he said, coolly. Then he asked, "Who do you intend to put in front of a judge? Moshid? There's no way you can do that. We can't allow that. It won't work, not if we're to do business. You do understand, don't you?"

"Yeah. I do now."

We crossed the jungle trail. He was a shape there, in the shadows, using that walking stick like a probe.

We found a piece of luminescent tape. I checked my GPS monitor. We weren't but ninety meters from the

THE WRONG SIDE OF BRIGHTNESS

mortar position. "Here," I whispered, pointing with the submachine gun.

"Do *you* want to lead?" he asked, gruffly.

"You'd be behind me with the pistol. . . . Let's hurry. We want to hit them right before dawn." I could see the faintest gray mottling above the tops of the trees, though not quite gray enough to totally erase the stars.

Martel picked up his pace. The game trail rose, weaved through the trees.

Then he stopped, and turned around, deliberately.

"Wait," he said. "You . . . Loflin. Were you in the desert with Nicholson?" I could see his white teeth, even in the darkness, through the netting. "Are you Ford? You saw Moshid kill a nurse, right? At the end of your desert *escapade?*" He was excited, like what he'd discovered earned him a Nobel prize in leverage.

"We don't have time to talk," I replied.

"You *are* Ford," he chuckled. "Oh, yes, this remarkable *earnestness* makes sense now. Nicholson and his French friend came to me for information a couple of years ago. Oh, I know more than you suppose." He chuckled again, a very odd delight. "Do you . . . do you still intend to take the bastard alive?" he asked.

"No," I lied.

"Good . . . good," Martel said. "A wise decision." I could tell he believed I was lying. He walked up the trail. Maybe I should handcuff Martel until this is over, I thought. Keep him out of this action. I could see Pildi had really screwed up. Martel was worried about what Moshid would say about the diamond business, say to a judge.

"You're silent," Martel said from in front of me.

I was silent. I was thinking. I saw everything going

to hell. Call it a theory—I had a theory. I saw where this could go. Such crap—

Then I didn't have time to think. Too much happened too quickly.

I heard distant engines, distant aircraft engines, a deep thrum that was there then disappeared. Then I distinctly heard three clicks over the radio, three breaks— our signal for trouble.

Then Martel stopped, froze right there in front of me. He took a step backward.

"Put the weapon down, Mr. Oliver, drop it to your feet," a deep baritone said, in English with a Creole French accent.

"Bonjour, Monsieur Oliver," another voice said from the bushes.

"Ariel?" Martel said, in fear and anger. "Ariel? I'll be damned!"

"Mr. Loflin!" another voice yelled.

"Ahtee?" I asked.

"Yes."

"Do not shoot, Mr. Loflin. It's all right."

"The weapon, Monsieur Oliver . . . please. Drop the pistol."

I could see Martel—or Oliver—hesitate.

"Ford," Oliver snapped. He stepped closer to me, the pistol still in his hand.

"I'm confused," I said, deliberately. I was drenched in sweat and shaking, but I had the submachine gun. God knows what kept me from opening up, other than discipline in uncertainty, other than I could see the shapes of three men rising from the bush, all wielding automatic rifles, and I could see Ahtee, standing in the trail, no weapon in his hands, but a tall black man wear-

ing camouflage fatigues and a beret at his side, the man
pointing a pistol at the former Mr. Martel.

"Ford!"

It was Pildi's voice, in the haze of the radio.

From the rush of static, so calm in the strange silence
of that jungle glade: "Ford—there's a change, Ford.
Reply."

I definitely heard the engines now, a huge prop transport of some sort, banking unseen in the gray sky above
the jungle.

"Damn straight there's a change," a deep voice
drawled behind me, a voice one mean notch beyond a
chuckle. "Ollie, you're refried *fromage,* boy."

Oliver swung around, in utter shock, despite the mottled light, I saw—through the net—the icy bleach of
his skin and the utter black of his gimlet eyes. *"Brune,"*
he breathed.

"You missed me. . . . Now I'm gonna bust *you,*
Ollie."

"You're here? With Moshid?"

"Not egg-zackly, Ollie."

"I knew you weren't dead."

"Now, don't jump to conclusions, Ollie. Ole Moshid
didn't double-cross you. He jes' fucked up and failed to
nail me."

"We can still do business."

"Bidnus cain't be bidnus anymore, Ollie."

Instantly Martel dove for the brush, the thick fronds
and tangle, but Brune and Ariel expected it. The muffled
shots from their silenced automatic pistols were like the
rapid clacks of car doors latching hard, *clackclackclack,*
orange muzzle blasts in the gray light and strangling

green of the jungle, the vague scent of cordite in the tepid, fetid air.

Ariel slid away from Ahtee, then stopped, staring down at Oliver's motionless body. A huge wall of camo fatigues—Jimmy Duke Brune, sweating, black bearded—stepped around me. He wore an Aussie bush hat and a headset radio rig, with the pencil mike a black plastic finger in front of his cracked pink lips. A plug of chewing tobacco put a loose ball in the middle of his left cheek. "Scuze me, Ford," he muttered, the chaw moving awkwardly as he spoke.

Now Brune stood over Oliver's body.

The tobacco chaw disappeared. Brune's head moved back and he spat, not on the body, but to the side of the trail, a long brown tobacco dart of spittle.

His eyes looked so white in the gloom, big, almost sad.

"You oughtta say sumpin', Ollie, sumpin' decent," Brune sniffed. "'Cept I know you don't even give a hoot about your own gawd-damned soul, since it ain't made ah diamond." Brune raised his pistol; then, as if remembering something, he moved the weapon from his right hand to his left and put his right thumb on his chest in the spot where his heart ought to be. I swear it, he crossed himself, thumb action, and as he did he glanced up at me—those eyes, brown-white gloom.

Now Brune took the pistol in his right hand, aimed the silenced automatic at the body, put a kill shot into Oliver's motionless head, one soft, ugly *fwack.*

Brune looked up again, straight at me. "Keep your mouth shut and your finger off the trigger, Ford," he said, and he said it softly. "This ends a bidnus between me an' him. You seed it but you ain't involved." Then he touched the earpiece of his radio headset, spoke into the tiny mike. "You got Major Pildi? . . . Put him on. . . . Major? How's your haid, huh? . . . Lemme apologize personally. I'd ah liked something different . . . Naw, just meet me at the fence . . . Right."

I FOLLOWED BRUNE OUT OF THE JUNGLE INTO THE opening on the rise. There was the mortar, emplaced, you could see it in the light. Roger sat beside it, smoking a cigarette, the other mortarman was in the bush, taking a crap.

The turboprop throb of the transport grew loud again.

"It's a Transall, Ford," Brune drawled. "Moshid thinks he's going to Congo, to meet some new bidnus men. He thinks we're kidnapping him's all. . . . But he ain't going to Congo. And we ain't kidnappers." Brune started walking down a game trail that widened. "Come on, Ford. Less head for the compound."

I walked behind him, the sun up now. Clearing my throat I asked, "Were you waiting for us?"

"We got tipped you were coming. Las' night. You made a sat phone transmission and shit, you gotta know, if people are looking for you they can get that kinda trackin' info fast. But in the bush, you guys are good, real good. You erase trail damn well. But she told us you were out here."

"She?"

"My girl." He turned his head, grinned a brown-toothed grin.

I didn't say anything.

Brune said, "You seem to know sumpin' of who I am."

"R. B. Guyton told me about you."

"Yeah?" He grinned, clearly impressed I knew Guyton.

"Where's Moshid?" I asked.

His big eyes widened. "We, uh, arrested him, two days ago. The men did."

"What did you arrest him for?"

"'Cause she wanted us to." Brune glanced at me. "My girl asked us to."

THE SUN WAS UP NOW, BRIGHT AND REFLECTING IN the clouds.

We reached the fence line, a wave of vine and brush in the razor wire and steel barbs.

At a break in the wire we met five more men, all of them wearing camouflage green and slash-brown jungle fatigues, each one with a black beret slouching on a shaved head, crossed bones but no skull on the beret's cap patch. One of the men, a fellow missing his left ear, was white, the other four were black. They were all rangy, straight-faced, dark-eyed.

We went through the cut. The dog on the nearest dog line barked once then quit. One of the men tossed the dog what looked like a dog biscuit.

I asked, "This a merc outfit you're with?"

"Them? Ariel's bunch? They're contract, but, you know, they're all French. Former Legionnaires." He glanced at me, like he wondered if I knew what that might mean. "And I ain't *with* them," he added, as if he couldn't believe I might conclude he was.

Yes, I had realized how little I actually knew. I

started to think about how stupid and irrational I'd been, but only started on it.

Here came the Transall, settling above the tree line, then dropping into the hidden jungle airfield.

We passed one of the half-buried quonsets. Three unshaven men I took to be Moshid's leaned against a stack of sandbags, three men with bored faces smoking and speaking to one another in Sango, the patois of the Central African Republic. One of the dogs — still chained to his line — had curled up at the entrance to the quonset hut. The dog's head rose as we passed.

"Where's Moshid stashed?" I asked Brune.

"Got him cuffed to his fucking safe," Brune replied.

I started to ask if I could talk to him but I didn't want Brune to say no.

Pildi's men filtered out of the jungle. They didn't look too upset at missing the firefight. They were smoking cigars and chatting. Except for Pildi — he walked through the break in the fence, arms folded. He scowled, a bright glare reflecting from his sunglasses.

The mercs hadn't disarmed Pildi's men, but there were four or five mercs watching them.

I said to Brune, "You aren't disarming us?"

"Think we should?" he replied. "I figure you're okay, least my girl says you're okay enough. Hell, we done your job for you. . . . Can I offer you sumpin' to drink?"

"It doesn't look like you had much of a fight when you took the place."

"We pulled a sort of Trojan Horse thang, came in with a supposed shipment of ammo from Su-dan. They weren't expecting nothing, they're all drunk. You want pros, you pay for pros. Moshid only had two, three bad

boys and we knew who they were and where they
were."

"Where are they now?"

He gestured toward the jungle. "Dead, out there.
They shoulda give him up."

Brune went to the porch of the leprosarium, pulled
two one-liter bottles of San Pellegrino water out of a
cooler. He passed me a bottle, with a twist of his wrist
took the cap off of his. Plywood and aluminum held up
the one remaining section of the leprosarium's roof,
strategically buttressed right above the entrance to
Moshid's bunker. Two mercs stood at the sandbagged
entrance, smoking, submachine guns slung over their
shoulders.

"You've talked to Moshid?"

Finishing his first, slaking hit of water, Brune said,
"Shoor. Oliver had him try to put me down. We talked
about how he screwed that up." Drops of water clung to
Brune's beard, glistening.

I opened my bottle, took a sip as Brune took another
long hit of fancy Italian water.

Brune carefully balanced the bottle on the rotten, de-
crepit rail of the porch, looked over at me. "Moshid was
funny, too, what he said to me as me and Ariel bust in
on him in bed, run the girl out the door. 'See, you're not
dead,' Moshid says, like I'm gonna ig-nore intent.
'You're safe, here,' he says, like I didn't have thirty
guys in control of the base. 'This is my world here, not
Oliver's,' he says. And I tell 'im, 'Yeah, you're god
here, man.' I mean, it was like he didn't have any idea
of what was happening to him." An odd glint slipped
into Brune's eyes. He reached for the water bottle again,
looked at the mouth, then said, "I been thinkin' about

what he was saying, too. This place," Brune gestured, pointing to the space in the jungle, using the green San Pellegrino bottle as if it were a wand, "—if everybody didn't know where it was already, it'd have possibilities. But like, you know, if the French wanted to put an air strike in here, we're thirty minutes by jet from Bangui. Get a laser over there in the wood line, guide that smart bomb in the door, and whammo, you piss one bunker. May as well be livin' in Paris, you know?" Brune took a sip of water, a small one this time, then added, almost philosophically, "Faced with those facts, if you are shippin' guns, may as well work out of Cyprus, right? Good Greek food, nekked Swedish gals on the beach? They got a lot better weather on Cyprus."

Brune put the empty bottle down. "Lemme tell you something else, in case you start thinkin' I'm settin' you up. Moshid was expectin' to hear from Oliver. Yeah, he said that. He thought Ollie was gonna fly in or something, not come out of the fucking jungle. But he said Ollie was coming, coming to conclude a deal. Here's how I read that. Ollie was playing you both ways. The fact he didn't rat you to Moshid means he'd decided you an' Pildi'd be okay in bidnus."

"So . . . Oliver knew Moshid was here? You're sure of that?"

"I'm just tellin' you what the man said. Moshid's always fulla bullshit. He coulda been tryin' to make a deal with me, like, he gives me Ollie and I forget he tried to help Ollie kill me. That sort of play don't work." Brune shrugged. "He still ain't figured what my gal wants him for." His teeth appeared, a flash of brown stain. "I'll go to great lengths, man, to impress a girl. 'Specially when

the cut's guaranteed and we don't have to deal with any
Belgian brokers."

THE JEEP FROM THE AIRSTRIP ARRIVED.
She wore sunglasses, the mantis lenses in the tropic
light an intense obsidian.

Dominique Cadeau was silent, barely glancing at
Brune as she slipped from the jeep. She wore a fawn-
colored jumpsuit, a green camouflage scarf.

Jimmy Duke stepped from the front porch, met her
near the entrance to the bunker. He pecked her on the
cheek.

I GUESS I HAD ABOUT A MINUTE-LONG LOOK AT
Moshid. They brought him out of the bunker, a frightened man in a gray jumpsuit.

What I wanted to say and what I could say were at
deep odds with what I could do.

So I watched. I watched Ariel drag the man by his
collar, watched the other two mercs hold his cuffed legs.

He didn't even twist and fight, that was over. And the
duct tape on his mouth squelched any comments. No,
they moved so quickly I didn't notice anything on his
hands, didn't see the diamond ring.

They didn't do it in the open space, they didn't do it
in front of television cameras live before a global audience. I started to follow them into the jungle but Jimmy
Duke put the back of his hand against my gut and said,
"This is private and you and me ain't in it. Not like she
is."

Dominique, three mercs, and Moshid disappeared

into the green. Two of the chained dogs barked, then quit barking.

THERE WAS NO PARTICULAR DRAMA IN THE TEN minutes they were gone. Jimmy Duke Brune drank another bottle of water. Tango chatted with two of the mercs about a friend who'd been killed in a battle over in the Congo. As I got a second bottle of water from the cooler, Pildi came over to me and said, "All of our costs will be recovered. Including yours."

"Forget the money."

"No," he insisted, "nineteen thousand carats of diamonds. Expenses will be recovered."

THE THREE MERCS RETURNED.

No one said anything when Ariel held up a severed finger, an index finger, with a diamond ring still on it. Ariel slipped the diamond ring off, then tossed the finger to one of the dogs. The dog sniffed it, growled, then left it there, whimpering. Someone else tossed the dog a biscuit.

She returned.

Dominique walked past Jimmy Duke Brune, started to get into the jeep, then turned and looked at me.

"He asked me why, Ford. And I told him, 'You killed my sister. You knew her in Iraq as Edira.' And he said, 'That French spy?' Those were his last words. Your fucking nurse," Cadeau said as she climbed into the jeep, "*my* sister."

"Why now?" I asked.

"I . . . I didn't know until Elise told me, after she left

you in Switzerland," Dominique said, so bitterly. "As far as *they* are concerned, I'm strictly operations."

Her hard little face clouded—but it went no further.

"Was your sister an agent, Dominique, working inside Iraq?"

"She was the best," Dominique replied with a touch of arrogance. "The best."

"What about the old men he killed, in that village?"

The jeep driver turned the motor over.

"What old men?" Dominique asked.

When I failed to reply, Dominique sat down in the passenger seat and adjusted her sunglasses.

The driver put the jeep in gear and with a lurch it headed for the airfield.

"Bye, honey," Jimmy Duke yelled.

CHAPTER 15

SHE ASKED ME, "ARE YOU SATISFIED WITH THIS, AS
it is?"

"How can I be satisfied?" I replied.

"*You* cannot be satisfied."

"Right, the romance of absolute statements . . . '*You*
cannot be satisfied.' Gimme a break."

"Don't mimic me."

"I'm not mimicking you. Do you want another glass
of wine?"

She reached for her empty glass, over on the night-
stand. I filled it.

"Careful," she said. "They'll make you pay for the
sheets."

"I'm not going to spill it."

"See, you're still angry."

"I'm not angry, Colonel. I'm tired."

"There are things I cannot say. It's my *business*." She took a sip of wine, fell silent.

I thought, as I lay there next to her, she's an intelligence agent, she's a goddamn spy, and the last thing I need is a lover who's a spy.

"Peter?" She gave her eyelashes a heavy bat.

Bat those eyelashes, baby, I thought, move those lips.

"Peter?"

"Yes."

"There were things you could not know," she began, starting that exculpatory spiel for the fifty-third time.

I let her talk, the fifty-fourth through seventy times seven times I let her try and explain herself. I took a certain, malicious delight in letting her try and untangle the lies, evasions, murder, and darkness, let her face the unresolved.

She fell silent.

"Do you want another glass of wine?"

"Of course."

I filled her glass.

Elise watched the deep red wine swirl into the crystal.

BACK IN THE STATES I SAW KILEAN, AT HIS HOUSE IN Annandale. He was out in the courtyard, a bottle of scotch on a tray table.

I told him about Moshid's base on the Chinko, about Dominique, about how it finished. As he listened the ambassador's gray eyebrows knit tighter and tighter, until they looked like cold gray screws pushing out of his face.

He took a long sip of scotch, just drained the glass.

I could see he was trying to relax, his version of trying to relax.

"What have you learned about Samir?" I asked.

"Nothing," Kilean replied. His had gripped the empty glass.

"We weren't involved," Kilean said, abruptly answering a question I hadn't asked. "You know we weren't involved."

He was standing by that marble statue, the one of the Greek boy, except he wasn't looking at it, he wasn't looking at me, either, and he wasn't looking at the oak tree, though a low branch almost clonked him on the head. Grim, the old boy was icy, screwed, and grim.

"You want another shot of scotch, Ambassador?"

"Great idea, Pete."

I picked the bottle up off of the tray, slopped a jigger's worth into his glass.

"Hold it, Pete, right there. I've already had close to enough."

"If that's too much let me get you another glass."

"No, that's fine."

"Ice?"

"No, neat's okay."

He took the glass, held it, his eyebrows still knit tight and distorting his face. That's when I noticed he had a faraway look in his eye, not bright but dim, a dead gem like the back side of a moon, the eye of slow suicide.

"We weren't involved," he said. And he repeated it again, muttering into the glass of scotch. "We weren't involved."

"I didn't ask," I snapped.

Now he looked at me, an old man in sudden shock.

IN NEW YORK—MAYBE A WEEK BEFORE I SAW
Kilean—I called Trish out in California, and on the
third try I managed to get through her secretary into her
corporate inner sanctum.

She took me on her speakerphone and I could hear
other voices in the background.

"Pete Ford," she said too brightly, "where have you
been?"

"The Central African Republic," I said.

"Not *again*," she replied. "Weren't you there a couple of years ago . . . or was that Uganda?"

RUE DE BIEVRE, PARIS. R. B. GUYTON WASN'T HOME.
Lissta was. She stood there, holding open that massive
wooden door, the one with the iron knocker.

"He's in Central America somewhere," she said,
cracking her chewing gum. "They got a bunch of Indi-
ans with guns and cell phones taking over a town. . . .
Coming in?"

"I'm in a rush, actually."

"Really? On your way to a fire?"

"I just wanted to say hello and drop off this pistol." I
gave her Nicholson's pistol.

She looked at the pistol, looked back at me. "You
look sorta pale," she observed. "You been sick?"

"I've got a date with a French intelligence agent."

"No kidding?" Lissta cracked her gum. "A he, a she,
or an it?"

"A she."

Lissta rolled her gum, asked, "Where you meeting
her?"

"At her apartment."

"It'll be bugged . . . won't it? I mean, don't spies bug other spies?"

"I don't intend to stay with her at her apartment."

"Oh? Where do you intend to go?"

"I'm going to take her to my hotel room."

"So . . . there *is* a fire."

DAMN IT, I'VE BLOWN IT. I GOT AHEAD OF MYSELF. I didn't want to finish like this, in fragments, leaping ahead, digressing, falling backward. I wanted this to end with the way I felt out there in Africa, the anger, heat, confusion, the letdown and loss. I wanted you to feel that, feel like I felt when I turned away from Jimmy Duke Brune and walked to the cut in the fence, went right through, and for three days sought the sanity of the jungle.

The sanity of the jungle—the Lord knows I'm nuts if I believe crap like that.

I guess Pildi and his men flew out with Jimmy Duke Brune and Ariel's mercs. I walked out. I sort of took the same route back we took in, except for a long tromp through the saw grass. This time I wanted to find an elephant, but I didn't even find elephant spoor.

When I reached the river I got one of the rafts, put it in the water, and I let it float. I watched the crocs. I swatted insects. I went through a downpour, a real afternoon Niagara. Maybe I shouldn't have done it but I floated at night, listening to the pleasant chaos of the jungle. Maybe I had a fever, but this fever was sane, the delirium lucid.

That night I tried to think about Elise, but it was too hot, too stifling. The air was a cloak, a warm, stifling

cloak on me, on the water's surface. Malaria? I was
shaking. Malaria? I took the tablets, man, I shouldn't
get malaria. Malaria? *Dear Christ, save me, I am sweating and shaking.* I grabbed my canteen, put it to my lips,
spilled the fresh water on my face, the tepid water on
my eyes, on my chest, the rippling current of the hot
river beneath my back—

IN THE MORNING I WOKE, THE HEAT ON MY FACE, THE
buzzing insect sound, a loud dragonfly above me.

I saw the dragonfly's shadow on the surface of
the river, a phantom hint of it, then it expanded, and the
sound expanded, and I looked up and saw the helicopter.

Pildi dropped a line from the open side of the chopper, a rescue loop on the end of the cable.

I couldn't hear his voice, but I could see his lips. "Put
it on," he screamed, though I couldn't hear the scream.

I slipped the rescue loop over my shoulders, felt the
tug almost immediately as the winch began the lift and
the helicopter rose.

In the chopper Pildi said with a shout, "You are *cray-
zee*. We've been looking for you for two days."

I shrugged. Why argue. I knew I was crazy.

Then Pildi said, "She's been trying to call you, on the
sat phone."

"Who?"

"Lieutenant Colonel Neaves."

"Where's she calling from?"

"Paris."

One of the Brit contract pilots handed me a bottle of
water. I drank it.

When I finished the water I said, "Pildi, where are we going?"

"After Kampala, I am flying to Dinkaland, to meet the Transall. Brune—well, he said that woman told him to be generous with us in the distribution of Moshid's weapons. . . . Nineteen thousand carats, Ford."

"You split that, too?"

Pildi nodded. "All costs were covered."

I looked down at the jungle. We were well beyond the river, heading southeast.

Then Pildi said to me, "You aren't going to Paris?"

"I don't know," I replied.

Pildi shook his head. "Ford," he muttered.

Then he took a seat near the open doorway—and muttered some more.

I sat there, glum, feeling the hard flow of the air from the rotorwash. My brow knit, my eyebrows coming together like two brown screws—

BUT IT DIDN'T FINISH LIKE THAT.

It should have ended out there in Africa, amid the anger, heat, the letdown and confusion.

But it didn't end, not out there.

It didn't end out there.